Soul

Short stories from the 2023
Mansfield Readers and Writers
short story competition

Published by Mansfield Readers & Writers Incorporated in 2024

www.mansfieldreadersandwriters.com
ISBN: 978-0-6457242-2-6 (paperback)

A catalogue record for this book is available from the National Library of Australia

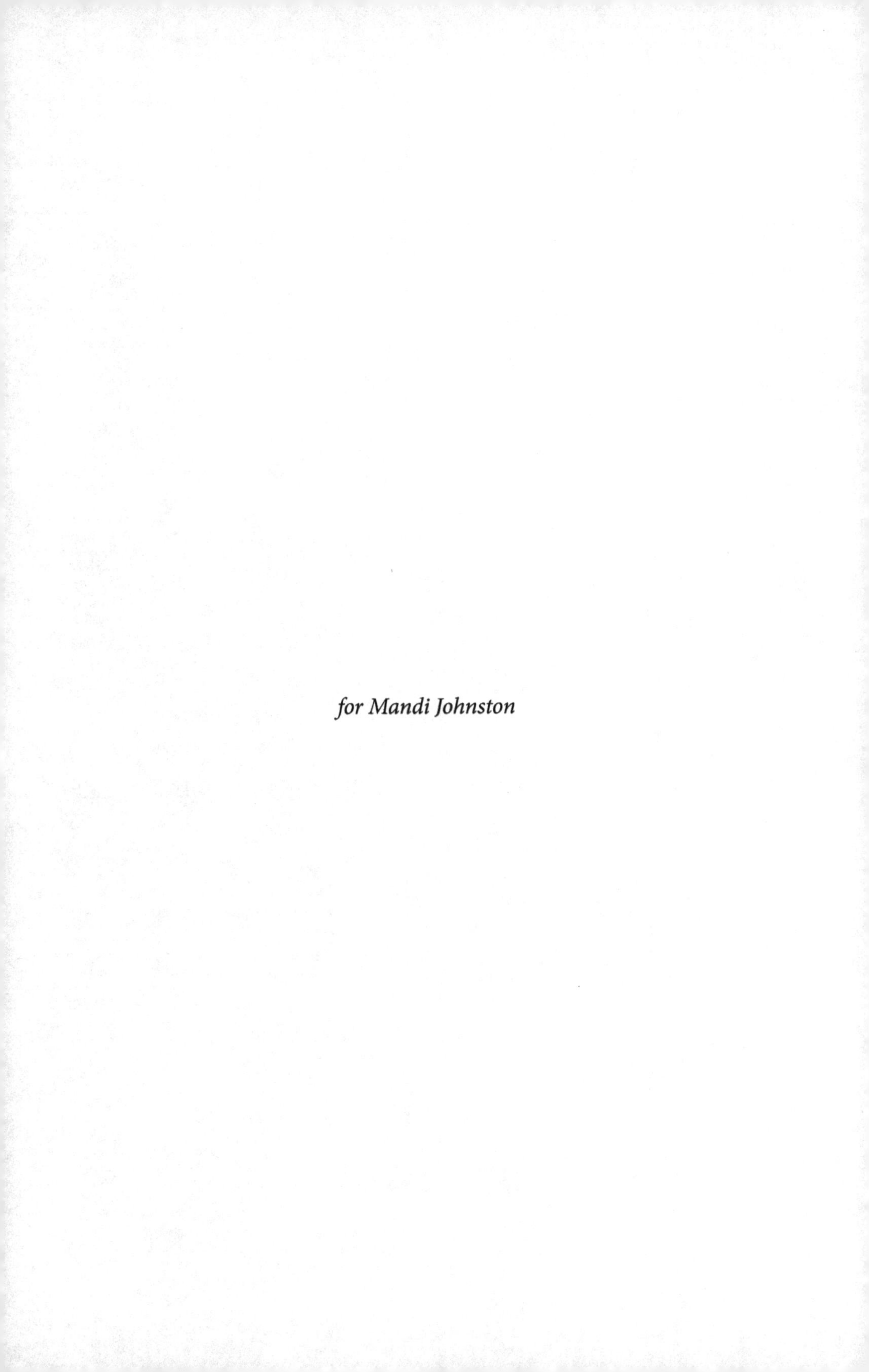

for Mandi Johnston

Mandi Johnston was one of the first people to join Mansfield Readers and Writers Inc. The family (Mandi, her husband Matt and sons Evan and Oscar) had bought a block and built a house at Tolmie. Mandi enthusiastically joined in community activities, getting involved in Tolmie Sports, the Mansfield Steiner School and then from June 2022 with Mansfield Readers and Writers.

Mandi brought her love of reading and literature to her involvement with Mansfield Readers and Writers. She also brought considerable experience in organising and running large projects. She had the best Excel spreadsheets any of us had ever seen, and she knew how to use them. With Mandi involved, we had tools that could help us bring our plan to life. Another thing that Mandi brought - and we only found this out after we'd known her for a while - was a dream she'd had for ages to be part of a writers' festival.

Most of all, Mandi brought herself, wholeheartedly. A woman with soul, and class. All the way. We were all better for knowing her.

Sadly, Mandi passed away in May 2023. We miss her still but her legacy remains. She reminded us to embrace life and follow our dreams.

Thank you Mandi.

Contents

Introduction

A short story anthology like *Soul* is the best sort of lucky dip. You might think that this year the stories would be tied together somehow – even if in diverse and endlessly interesting ways – because they respond to the theme of 'soul'. You'll be surprised, though. There's a delicious diversity here and a reminder that every writer brings their unique self to their storytelling.

Supporting and providing opportunities for writers and readers is at the core of what Mansfield Readers and Writers does. For this reason, we asked Laura E. Goodin to run two short story courses for us before entries closed, to give new and emerging writers in particular the opportunity to work on their story one more time before submitting.

Laura's workshops were really good. If you're writing short stories, and you get a chance to attend one of them, I'd highly recommend them.

Yet very few writers attended. I'll be honest - many of the writers who submitted stories this year would have benefited from the workshop.

Interestingly, a large percentage of those who did attend are being published – here or in other short story collections or with larger works. 'I'm not sure of the exact correlation between the workshops we offered and the publication elsewhere. What it says though, is that the writers who get their work accepted are the ones who understand that there is always room for improvement; always something to learn that will help you be a better writer and help to get your short story to the next shining level.

After all, the thing about short stories is that there is nowhere to hide. Every. Word. Counts. Every piece of punctuation. Every line break. Every lexical choice. Every idea and object must work to support the story. A short story has an intensity that is rarely found in longer forms like novels.

What we saw in the submissions that came through this year's short story competition was a wide range of 'completedness'. Our esteemed judge Laurie Steed saw it too, and if there was a theme from our side of the desk it was 'I wish this had had just a little bit more work'.

*

The authors of the stories in the *Soul* anthology have done the work, and written stories that align with this year's rather abstract theme.

After all, what is soul? When we came up with the theme we were mainly thinking about the perfect pairing of 'heart and soul', almost cliché, except that we had put a lot of both those qualities into everything we'd done since forming Mansfield Readers and Writers in 2022. We imagined these two anthologies sitting side by side on a shelf, titles complementing each other and providing a hint of the dedication that has gone into not only writing the stories but also reading, longlisting, shortlisting and publishing them. Truly an example of 'heart and soul'.

All of us at Mansfield Readers and writers hope you enjoy this anthology of stories. It will look wonderful on the shelf beside your copy of 2023's *Heart*.

Miriam Zolin
Short Story Convenor, Mansfield Readers and Writers

Judge's Report

Laurie Steed

It has struck me that not everyone is as committed to the short story form as I am.

I should be heartbroken by this. I'm actually over the moon. Why does this excite me? Well, put frankly, it means it's increasingly a form for the most dedicated, committed writers, those who see not their name in glittering lights but the thought of an exquisitely executed short story as the main event.

There were some great stories in this year's Mansfield Readers and Writers Short Story Competitions and, quite frankly, some baffling ones, too. You will thankfully find the great ones in this anthology. They made it by paying attention to logic, anchoring in specificity and authenticity, leaning into complexity over simplicity, and realising that it's the cocking of a gun that's sometimes much more powerful than the gunshot.

The winning story in this year's local category was 'Small Town God', and it's a ripper, easily holding its own alongside the other shortlisted stories in 2023. It's told from the POV of a female high school student and embedded with authentic, age-appropriate dialogue. The use of a phone charger as a flirtation device is particularly inspired, and a sense of longing permeates every word and makes this a deeply memorable story.

The winning story in the open category was 'Dust'. This is one of those rare cases where a writer has chosen a profoundly familiar subject (dementia) but made it their own thanks to deft use of humour, pathos, and honesty. The family depicted in 'Dust' is imperfect, and this heartfelt, deeply moving story is better for their flaws, failings and vulnerability.

Other shortlisted stories included 'The Sense of Endings', 'Mouse in Paris' and 'Wife in Silhouette'. While each of these stories left me wanting just a tiny bit more, they also took a complex and more challenging road at each turn and should be commended for their willingness to think outside the box. 'The Sense of Endings' by Kristof Mikes-Liu is a clever, well-measured story about parental responsibility from both a mother and son as the former realises she's losing control of the boy who once so profoundly needed her care and guidance. 'Mouse in Paris', by Jodie Kewley, is a deeply thoughtful, quietly powerful meditation on siblings, grief and responsibility played out in one of the world's most aesthetically beautiful cities Finally, 'Wife in Silhouette', by Kamille Roach starts a little too sweetly but moves quickly into the evocative and emotionally compelling when a wife returns just after her death, albeit in a different form, to comfort her still grieving husband.

Congratulations to all those writers shortlisted for this year's awards. To those who weren't in contention this time, my advice is deceptively simple. Never settle for a good story when a great one could be waiting on the back of another draft or more careful revision.

Laurie Steed, December 2023

Dust

Deborah May

'Dust' is the winning story in the 2023 Mansfield Readers and Writers short story competition

'He'll have to be buried in his pyjamas,' Mum says. 'I've gotten rid of all his clothes. I didn't think.' She has a crazed look on her thin face - one I haven't seen since I stopped going to family Christmases. She stands on tiptoe to kiss my cheek. She's the only person whose kiss can make you feel colder and more alone. My brother Matt once compared it to being pecked by a frozen chicken.

She's emptied out Dad's room of the last two years, leaving it as impersonal and beige as a hospital ward. Gone are the picture books and jigsaw puzzles we brought into the Memory Care unit to entertain him, those clacking magnetic balls from the Australian Geographic store that amused him for a while, the family photos Blu-tacked to the wall.

The stretcher bed set up for mum is neatly made and pushed back against the wall. The ensuite cupboard that's usually locked is open. Dad's razor, shampoo and the massive container of hand sanitiser have gone.

Mum's long grey hair is tied in a straggly ponytail instead of the neat low bun she usually wears and her stockings have a ladder in them.

Dad's asleep on his back with his mouth open, a mustard brown washcloth next to his face for when he coughs or dribbles, the bedclothes tucked up around his chin. I kiss his hot forehead. His stubble is turning into a full beard. It must really be over if Mum's letting him go unshaven.

'He hasn't opened his eyes at all today,' says Mum. 'But at least all that horrific coughing has stopped. They say it won't be long now.'

'What if he wakes up and sees you've taken away all his things?'

'He's not going to wake up.'

I can't help wondering if it's my fault. They say it's pneumonia brought on by a bladder infection, but what if it isn't? What if it's pneumonia brought on by inhaling a piece of bread into his lungs when I insisted they let him have a sandwich instead of the brown goop that looked like wet cat food they'd been feeding him? Mum's repeatedly told me not to interfere in his care, but I couldn't bear the way his hungry eyes followed the sandwich cart.

In any case, whatever caused it, there is to be no hospital, no X-rays and no doctors besides Dr. Wilson who eases the residents into death with benevolent indifference.

'Pneumonia is a blessing compared to a slow death from cancer,' Mum told me over the phone a few days ago. 'They call it the "old man's friend."'

Six months ago Dr. Wilson decided after preliminary tests that Dad had bowel cancer, although again, he didn't investigate further to confirm it, because what would be the point in subjecting Dad to frightening examinations and surgery?

'He has to be buried in a suit,' I say now, not sure why it matters so much that Dad's not sent off in his striped flannel pyjamas from Kmart. 'Let me get him one.'

'If you insist,' Mum says graciously. 'But it would be good to get it today, so that we're organised.' Then she adds as I head out the door, probably worried that she's given me too much authority, 'But no more asking the staff if they can call an ambulance for your father.' Her voice rises as I start down the hall. I dodge some witches hats placed around a wet patch on the blue carpet as she calls, 'It's not your place to discuss his care.'

Not your place. Her words sting like a hard slap as only a mother's can as I walk down the hall to the security door.

As I try to type in the code to exit, Malcolm, a new resident, lurks next to me, trying to see what I'm doing.

'How's it going?' I ask. He smiles and nods, moves closer to the sliding glass door, ready to make a run for it when it opens.

Benji, one of the carers, comes and leads him away with a firm hand on his elbow and a promise of a cup of tea. 'It's best not to interact with Malcolm,' he tells me over his shoulder, as if it's my fault. 'He can be a bit aggro.'

Dad tried to escape in the beginning too, even managed to break the keypad off the wall in a fit of frustration. Once he managed to escape by following someone who assumed he was a visitor. Security camera footage showed Dad sprinting up and down the street and around the car park, with three carers in tow before he got puffed out and let them lead him inside. He was laughing the whole time as if it was a game of chasey in a schoolyard.

After a few weeks he settled down. 'He's become institutionalised,' Phoebe the practice manager told us, as if Dad's lethargy was a win.

'He's become medicated, more like it,' said Matt when I told him. It's been a long time since Dad's been able to manage anything more than a sleepy shuffle.

The outside air smells especially fresh after the stuffiness of the nursing home and I breathe deep. Across the car park a young girl wraps silver tinsel around the stair railing of the orange brick meeting hall in readiness for the Sunday School Christmas party this evening.

Matt and I spent a large chunk of our youth in that hall. Each Sunday we had an hour of Sunday School followed by a two hour church service. Bookend that with a forty-five minute drive each way and that was the Sundays of our childhood. Then top that with the Friday and Saturday evenings of Youth Groups and Bible Studies, all designed to stop us from being corrupted by 'outside influences.' Lot of good it did.

Now half the people who I remember dressed in their Sunday best are Dad's fellow inmates in the aged care home which is run by the church. I bump into old Sunday School friends, people I thought I'd never have to face again, visiting their parents and we greet each other with mutual, although distant sadness.

I head up the Monash freeway to Chadstone, glad to be able to do something for Dad at the same time as getting away from Mum. The shopping centre car park is crawling with cars. I head straight to the farthest corner without bothering to find a closer spot. It's not a day to be optimistic.

It feels surreal to be in a shopping centre, floating through the festive atmosphere in a bubble of sadness. The upbeat Christmas music sounds like a sick joke.

I loiter like a shoplifter in Myer Menswear, rebuffing offers of assistance, interrupting one guy who tries to tell me about their free tailoring service. I tell him that hem length won't really matter and he shuts up, although he looks like he has more questions.

Poor Dad has been wearing pants that have shrunk above his ankles for two years because the track pants he wears for easy toileting assistance don't withstand the rigorous washing and drying process of the home.

I choose a shirt, a pale purple I know Mum won't like but Dad would love, and a darker purple tie. At the register I see some socks with a golf club pattern and I grab those too. I imagine Dad's pleasure if he could see them. This is the last time I will ever buy something for my father.

I pull out my ex-partner's credit card. Maybe I'm taking advantage of Rodney's remorse about leaving me, knowing he was taking with him my last chance to ever have a child. The thing is, I've been working part-time in a bookshop since I moved back to Melbourne while waiting to start teaching again next year so things are a little tight.

It's a lovely suit,' the elderly gent at the register says as he zips up the garment bag. 'I hope he enjoys it.' He is wary; seems a bit repulsed by my mournful demeanour and the mascara rings under my eyes.

It is a lovely suit - charcoal wool, ridiculously pricey. It's more expensive than any suit Dad would have worn in life but he'll enter the hereafter, if there is one, in style.

I was four when I learned about death. I was sitting in church fixated on an older girl called Susan because she was wearing her turquoise velvet suit covered with a repeating pattern of poodles on it. Damn, I loved that suit. I couldn't take my eyes off it and Mum kept tapping me to make me turn around and face the front.

Dad was giving the exhortation that day, looming over the podium which was too low for him. He didn't really need the microphone. I heard him say in his booming voice, 'Just as Adam and Eve were created from dust, so too to dust shall we return when we die and we shall remain dust until Jesus comes back to set up his kingdom.'

Dad was an excellent public speaker, much better than the other brethren who stammered as they read their over-rehearsed talks. Dad could have been a radio presenter with that voice.

I sat through the rest of the service with a burning ball of terror in my throat but I knew if I made a sound I'd get dragged in disgrace down the aisle to the cry room, which is where Matt often ended up because he couldn't resist kicking the underside of the seat in front of him. Whenever I saw Susan's poodle suit after that, I just thought of dust.

I wait for Matt in the street outside the home, as he told me to. 'I don't want to walk in there alone,' he'd texted, as if people will be waiting to try and convert him when he steps foot on the premises. The late afternoon air smells of sun-warmed flowers and mown grass.

'Well you look like shit,' he says, climbing out of the convertible he's rented to drive from the airport. He gives me a hug.

'So do you.' I squeeze him tight. Dad used to joke that if I cut my hair no one would be able to tell us apart. We both have Dad's unusually tall, shapeless build and facial features that look like we belong behind the bar of a British country pub, as I overheard one of my uncles say once. Even though Matt's two years older than me, people used to assume we were twins.

'Mum engineered a miracle getting Dad in here after what he did,' says Matt as we walk down the ramp.

'All her years of volunteering finally paid off. How could they say no?' If anything needed doing Mum was the person to ask, from playing piano for church services, to arranging fundraisers, to helping with the dinner service in the home three days a week. I think it was her way of compensating for her children, and eventually, her husband too.

It's nap hour, where they turn the lights down low and everyone dozes in place; drooping in armchairs, slumped over the dining tables, mouths agape. The lights on the Christmas tree have been turned off.

On the door of each room is a laminated photo of the occupant and a bio. Matt reads Dad's aloud. *'Barry has a wife, Ruth, a daughter Sarah, and a son, Matthew. Barry was an English and History teacher and ran his school's drama department. He now enjoys walking and looking at books about travel.*

'Nothing about the years he ran off with the receptionist from the high school or how he turned his back on the church after forcing us to spend our childhood neck deep in it,' he says.

There's a gold star stuck next to Dad's name, like the kind I'd get on my Sunday School homework. Over time I realised the colours of the stars were allocated to residents based on how easy or difficult they were to manage. The placid residents have gold whereas the challenging ones like Malcom have red. Dad's has changed over the two years he's been here as he's become weaker and meeker.

Two health care workers come out of Dad's room wheeling a laundry trolley and smile at us, tight-lipped. I imagine it's because Mum's told everyone not to discuss Dad's health with me.

A moment before I open the door I fantasise that Dad will be awake and sitting up in bed. After all, this isn't the first time he's been unwell that Mum's told me to prepare myself. But when we open the door he's still asleep, although somehow they've managed to put him in fresh pyjamas and change the sheets.

Mum's in a chair by the window. 'He won't know who you are, love,' Mum warns as Matt kisses her on the head.

'Well that's nothing new,' Matt says in the snarky way he's perfected over the years. He sits on the edge of Dad's bed.

'Hello Dad,' he says loudly in a jovial tone. 'What are you doing in bed at this hour of the day?' He grasps Dad's hands which have been placed neatly on his chest, brings them up to his lips and kisses them. 'It's Matt. Your wayward son.'

'Oh for heaven's sake, Matt,' says Mum. 'He can't understand a thing you say.'

Matt clears his throat. 'He looks so different. He's so skinny.' On Matt's last quick visit down from Sydney six months ago we took Mum and Dad to Montsalvat and had fish and chips by the Yarra on the way home. It was a perfect day until I missed an exit on a large roundabout, had to go around a second time and Dad threw up.

'I wish you could have spent more time with him when he was in here,' I say to Matt.

Mum says over my head, 'Sarah prefers him this way. She didn't bother with him for years; as soon as he came in here, she's here twice a week.'

Matt smiles sympathetically at me - we're both guilty of giving up on Mum and Dad during our twenties and thirties, although it's fair to say that they gave up on us first.

But here's the thing about Dad with advanced dementia: all I've had to do to please Dad for the last couple of years is smile at him and his face lights up like sunshine. Holding Dad's hand when I took him for walks was oddly familiar and comforting. It took me back to when I was a little girl, before the resentment and disillusionment took over, before he used to shout at me that I needed to have a good hard look at my life because I wasn't on the right path. I knew he meant the path to salvation because saving our souls was all that mattered in our house.

But now with all that behind us, it was just the simple bond of father and daughter again.

When Rodney left me eight months ago, instead of going to stay with Matt in Sydney like I usually would after a romantic disaster, I drove from Albury to Melbourne to visit Dad.

'Well *that* hurts,' said Matt when I told him where I was going. Mum and Dad disliked Rodney. He once told them that he was an atheist and that their church was a cult.

I sat at a table with Dad doing jigsaws. I talked, told him the truth, for perhaps the first time in my adult life. Of course he couldn't understand my words, but he could sense my sadness. Every now and then he'd reach across the table and pat my hand. It was just what I needed.

'He's so lovely to be around now,' I say.

'That's because he has no idea who you are,' says Mum.

'Of course he does. Just a couple of weeks ago I was taking Dad for a walk and Malcom, that new guy, the one who wears the Akubra, was yelling and Dad put his arm around me and pulled me away from him.'

'You weren't there, Mum?' asks Matt.

'No. Sarah always tries to visit when she knows I'm not here,' says Mum, looking up from the biblical crossword she's doing on her iPad. 'She's stopped filling in the visitors' log so she thinks I have no way of knowing, but people tell me.'

'I do wish I'd seen Dad more over the last few years,' says Matt. 'I imagine the talk of me being destined for eternal damnation would have stopped after he ran off with Mrs Shepherd.'

We *never* speak of those years. I'm always glad of Matt's willingness to have my back, but this is too much. I stretch my foot toward him and kick his ankle.

'He hasn't been himself for years,' says Mum,'It started long before his words went, you know.'

'You think his leaving you was because of dementia?' asks Matt .

'He hadn't been himself *for years*.' Mum repeats. 'Neither of you would know because you weren't around.'

'She had to get that dig in,' says Matt in an aside to me, rolling his eyes.

'You're both overgrown babies,' says Mum impatiently. 'It wasn't as if we asked for much. It's not as if living a life away from the Truth has worked out well for either of you.'

It was clear what was expected of Matt and I when we were growing up. We were to do our Bible readings, two Old Testament chapters and one New Testament chapter, every day. We were to get baptised, in an old bath tub hauled up onto the stage in the meeting hall, when we turned eighteen. At around twenty-two we would marry someone from the ecclesia, probably someone we were already distantly related to by marriage. But things hadn't gone according to plan.

I know Matt's tossing up whether to mention Adam, his partner of the last decade, but he lets it go.

'Dad did seem happy when I was here,' he says eventually. 'I wouldn't have said he was sick of living, put it that way.'

'You need to think about who he was before - how independent and proud he was,' Mum says. 'Would *that* man have wanted to live like *this?*'

'But that's only because he didn't know that he could still be happy here,' I say.

'He would have hated you spending all your time here, infantalizing him. He clearly and repeatedly told me when he got his dementia diagnosis that he didn't want his life prolonged once he couldn't look after himself.'

'Yes Lucy, weren't you brought up to respect other people's choices?' asks Matt jokingly.

Mum pretends she doesn't hear him.

We didn't get much information when Dad returned to Mum after a five-year absence. I rang to check on her one rainy Tuesday day a few years ago and Dad answered the phone. He had trouble talking. He hesitated and stammered before Mum took the phone from him.

She told me that Dad had started having trouble with his words; nouns especially hovered out of reach. Then one day he got up in class and everything that came out was gibberish. His class thought he was having a stroke and someone ran to get the principal. After a few tests, he was diagnosed with frontotemporal dementia.

'How long has he been back for?' I asked reeling from all this information. 'Oh I don't know,' said Mum. 'Could you please let Matt know? I hate to be the bearer of bad news.' I assumed she was talking about Dad's dementia, not his return.

Dad never returned to the classroom, only to Mum. We don't know if Mrs Shepherd left him, or he her. We never even met Mrs Shepherd. We only knew what had happened because Matt had a friend who taught at the same school as Dad. We were so angry with him during the Mrs Shepherd years we'd limited ourselves to emails and sporadic texts.

Matt was more angry at Dad for his hypocrisy than for the pain he'd caused Mum. I was torn about what upset me most but it was so bizarre I could almost pretend it wasn't happening if I didn't have to see it.

Things weren't the same when he came back, although we all pretended they were. He'd lost his self-confidence and become silent, not wanting to talk in case he couldn't finish what he had to say.

Dad never went back to church - I don't know if it was because he was unwelcome, too embarrassed, or if he'd had enough of the 'fanatical clan,' as his mother used to call it. Dad's joining the church when he met Mum in the seventies had caused as much conflict with his parents as Matt's and my non-allegiance had created with ours.

We were willing participants for the first eleven years or so of our lives. Then we started wishing that we could be normal - only go to church at Christmas or Easter like our school friends. When my friends came over to the house - something that only happened when mum wasn't home, I hid my Bible in my bottom drawer. If Matt and I wanted to play mix tapes of songs taped off the radio on our little cassette player, they were drowned out by Mum practicing hymn accompaniments on the piano. Hymns were the soundtrack of our youth, when we wanted it to be George Michael and Red Hot Chili Peppers.

There's a kind of sanctimonious hostility emanating from the polite women in knee-length skirts who pop in to check on Mum throughout the early evening. You can tell they want to say to me and Matt, *Don't you know how much pain you've caused your parents?* They'll go away and talk about how sad it is that our souls couldn't be saved over cups of tea and sponge cake. I know this because it's the kind of conversation I grew up hearing.

Outside Dad's door we hear the bustle of dinner time. Matt ducks out and brings back some sandwiches on a plastic plate. I can't eat them.

Through the window which looks onto the car park, we watch people arriving for the Sunday school party.

'Are those girls wearing *jeans*?' I ask.

'Oh yes,' says Mum. 'You can wear anything these days - one way of trying to retain the young ones. It's ghastly.'

'Mum you should go home and have a shower,' I say. 'We'll stay with Dad.'

'No thank you. I'll shower tomorrow.' It's as if she thinks we're going to abandon Dad the minute she leaves the room. Or perhaps she's worried I'll ring an ambulance, or bundle Dad into my car.

We open the window so Dad can hear the children singing, accompanied by the drone of cicadas.

I used to love standing up on stage with my Sunday school class in my best frock to perform our chosen song. Matt would usually be lectured all the way home for making silly faces or trying to make his classmates laugh when they were supposed to be singing.

When darkness falls and the home becomes silent, I accept that it's over, that Dad's not going to wake up again, that there'll be no miraculous recovery, no ambulance or hospital or capable doctors telling us that they can save him.

At around one o'clock Mum crashes on the stretcher bed. 'It's hard to tell who looks worse,' Matt says looking from her to Dad. The fluorescent light coming from the bathroom makes us all look haggard.

Matt and I google what death is like to try and get a sense of what will happen, holding our phones in one hand while holding one of Dad's hands in the other.

Maybe Dad will give us a sign, a parting gift, so we know that there's something after death.

'People who have near death experiences say they float above the room looking down,' suggests Matt. 'So don't let him see you crying when he goes, just in case. He hated seeing you upset.'

There's a deep snort and rattle. We look at Dad, alarmed and then realise it's coming from Mum. 'Well at least we now know why Dad left,' whispers Matt.

We start giggling like naughty kids in a quiet classroom, silently at first and then with shrieks and gasps until the horror of laughing at our father's deathbed hits us and our giggles dissolve into shamed silence.

'What if he heard us?' I ask.

'I think mum's snoring would have drowned us out,' says Matt and we start laughing again before getting control of ourselves.

'We're horrible children,' Matt says wiping his eyes.

'We need to make more of an effort with Mum, before she ends up in here herself.'

'Agreed,' whispers Matt. 'Maybe Adam and I will stay in Melbourne for Christmas. You in?'

'Sure,' I say, 'Although I feel sorry for Adam already.'

Looking at my frail sleeping parents, it seems ridiculous that we've let them become the monsters of our adult lives.

It could just be because I'm exhausted, but my brain starts to play tricks on me. The man in the bed no longer looks like Dad, his skin seems to be smoothing out and his features take on different shapes. I start to wonder if there's been some trick, that Dad has been replaced by someone else. His watery eyes are partly open but they're not looking at anything.

I think of all the times I let Dad down, the awful things I said to him the day I moved in with my boyfriend, all the times I didn't take his calls because I didn't want to hear what he had to say, how I never rang him to see how he was when he left Mum. I think of the flimsy excuses Matt and I made to avoid birthdays, Fathers' Days, Christmases.

'Don't think of those things,' says Matt, when I try to articulate it through sobs. 'I try not to. Think of the good things - how proud he was that you became a teacher like him; the nice times you shared together - how you made his time in this hellhole more bearable.'

'I'll try,' I dig through my pockets for an unused tissue.

'You know what I'm thinking of?' says Matt. "I'm thinking of Dad reading us stories at bedtime, after we'd done our Bible readings of course, how he always did the voices and put so much into it, how he'd go to the school library and borrow books he thought we'd like to read.'

'He did too,' I say. 'I remember that.'

'Where the hell are all the staff?' asks Matt. It seems like hours since they checked on us. Dad's breathing has changed. It's become heavier, more laboured.

'He was supposed to have more morphine by now,' I say. 'What if he's in pain?'

I race out to find someone. There's no one in the office. The whole living area is empty but then a white ghost rises up out of an armchair facing Dad's door. I jump before I realise that it's Martha, one of the carers, who's been napping in a chair covered by a sheet.

'I'm sorry,' she says, 'I needed a nap but I wanted to stay out here in case Malcolm tried to bother you. He wanders.'

'Dad was supposed to have more morphine at two.'

She takes her phone out of her apron pocket. It casts shadows on her sleep-creased face. 'I'm so sorry,' she says, 'I'll get the nurse.'

When I go back to the room, Matt is gently shaking Mum's shoulder to wake her while still hanging onto one of Dad's hands.

Dad's breathing has changed again, sped up as if it's approaching the end.

Mum gets up, and takes the hand of Dad's that I'd been holding for hours. I'm left with nothing to hang on to so I stand at the end of the bed and hold his foot through the bed sheet. 'I love you Dad,' I say, hoping just once he'll understand what I'm saying. I imagine his voice saying 'I love you too, Darl.'

But instead he just stops breathing. There's no more breath.

'That's it,' I say before I double over, winded like I've been punched in the gut.

'Quick,' says Matt, grabbing my arms and standing me up. We look up at the roof. 'Bye Dad,' we call, turning and waving to every section of the ceiling, as cheerily as if we're driving away after a weekend visit. 'Love you.'

But there's no feeling of him in the room at all. There's no sense of calm; nothing. It's just that one minute he was here, and now he isn't.

Mum is still talking to him and seems to have not realised that he's gone.

There's a knock on the door and I open it, expecting it to be Martha, arriving too late with the morphine. It's Malcolm. He steps into the room and takes in the scene: Mum softly talking to Dad, Matt crying in the corner, me holding the door open, having no idea what to do, and Malcolm knows. His face changes to one of sympathy and apology. He frowns, puts a hand to his chest and backs out of the room. I swear there's tears in his eyes.

A moment later a loud sigh escapes Dad's body and it sounds exactly like the exasperated groan he used to give when Matt and I were being silly or when nothing he seemed to do for Mum was good enough.

It is the perfect last word.

Small Town God

Molly Dunn

'Small Town God' is the winning local story in the 2023 Mansfield Readers and Writers short story competition

People talk about the escape, the release from reality. But I don't think reality is something we've ever experienced. Our lives - our small, hopeful lives - are buffered and bashed into something that slips past expectation. We pick a single layer of ourselves and call it real, brushing off the others as though they don't surround it, bury it, with their weight. Sometimes these layers are suffocating, and you can't breathe past all the history. Sometimes you feel empty, like everything within you is more than yourself. As though you're perfectly, helplessly insignificant.

We stood huddled beneath the locker bays, jumpers zipped above our noses and water clinging to our eyelashes and the tips of our hair. Fingers trip over phone screens as the rain drives the dry from the earth. His voice is muffled by the group of boys surrounding him, but I still catch his smile straining against lips numb with cold, his sharp laugh. The bell goes, but as the rest of us shuffle towards the classrooms, he remains standing by the lockers a moment longer, defiance - even in such a small act - written across his body. Eventually, he puts his head down, shoves his hands deep into his pockets and joins the swarm of students, disappearing into the ghosting rain.

Jodie bats at my arm, and my pen skitters across the page, drawing an ugly line through the words I've just written. She flicks her eyes to a spot behind me, a subtle order to look. The teacher is speaking in a low voice, chin tucked into his chest as he stares down at the figure hunched over the desk. He speaks with a kind of weary patience, a well-rehearsed monologue of which every word causes the boy to bridle further. Finally, Jim pushes his chair back, slides his laptop off the table and moves towards the door, dangerously quiet. A boy in the corner puts his hand up, and the teacher nods at him to speak.

'But, sir,' he starts defensively, 'What did he do?'

The teacher's face crumples as he looks at the boy, and the class begins to mutter their agreement. I stay silent, staring at the mark on my page.

'He was disrupting the class.'

'But how?'

'I don't have to explain myself to you.'

My gaze lifts to the window, snags on the boy leaning against the wall of the opposite building, face twisted in a discernible expression.

He walked into school the next day with a certain swagger. Passing me in the corridor, he met and held my gaze, widening his eyes ever so slightly. Daring me to look away. My mouth kicked up in an awkward smile and I looked down at my shoes, and he kept walking. I felt, somehow, as though I had failed a test. A challenge. My friend fell into step beside me, and he was gone.

He passed me again at the lockers later that day, and I felt something flutter in my stomach. The feeling gripped me, and I tried to meet his eye. To hold his stare, as he had held mine. But he was moving too fast, sprinting, weaving in and out of the clusters of students, huddled with their backs to the grey, misting world. They turned to watch him as he passed, watch his friends, close on his heels, all of them laughing. Always laughing.

'Okay okay okay, I've got news.' She began, and I grinned.

'Oooh yes, tell me.' I could've kicked myself for the false enthusiasm, how forced it sounded. Something hardened in her face, and I scrambled to recover the conversation.

'Sorry, that came out weird. I'm so tired, Wednesdays are the worst.'

Jodes brushed it off, leaning closer.

'Well… alright, so, basically, Jim was flirting with me. Like, nonstop. All class. He asked to borrow my charger, for one thing, which is weird cause he always asks to borrow yours. So…'

She flicks her eyebrows up in silent, suggestive question, and I suck at my teeth.

'Do you think he likes you?'

'Do you?'

'Sounds like it.'

She grinned, triumphant. Everyone loved Jim; you couldn't help it. There was a fear there, too - he existed on another plane. He was a legend, the son of a legend, and had known his place in this town since the moment he was born here. He was irritable, and quiet, and small; he was wry, and boisterous, and the center of everyone's universe.

I started looking out for him as our bus drove past his empty road, again. And again. Finally, one day, there he was. Sitting on that struggling scatter of grass at the intersection to Mitchell's Road, propped up against his backpack, a state of complete stillness.

I was tracing patterns in the fog on the window, swirls through the white which brought the world beyond into sharp clarity. I saw him look up, mark the bus approaching. Saw him stand, backpack gripped tightly in one hand and take a step towards the road. Something was different today. Every step onto the bus carried a weight, and he dropped into the seat closest to the front. I studied his face in the mirror, and noted the distant flatness in his eyes. Noted it, although I didn't know what it meant. The bus stopped, and I slid out from my seat, traipsing down the long aisle, caught in a parade of checkered skirts and windstoppers. Off the bus, I lengthened my stride, until I was keeping pace with him. He turned his head towards me, surprise - disbelief - causing the darkness in his eyes to gutter. I opened my mouth, closed it. Grimaced.

'Are you okay?' I wanted to ask. Nearly did, but something stopped me. The impossibility, perhaps, of bridging that gap. I shook my head, shrugged, and dropped back once more.

'God, that was awkward.' I muttered, exhaling heavily. Already thinking about how I'd tell my friends, laugh about it with them. The bell went, and I wandered towards the classrooms, watching the fragile blades of grass bend and bleed under my feet.

'Hey, can I have your charger?'

I push it towards the edge of the desk without looking up, and wait for him to leave. But he doesn't. Instead, he grabs my book, examining the lines upon lines of neatly distributed ink. He blows out a breath, flicking his eyes up and holding my gaze before I have time to look away. His eyes widen - just a little. Just enough to mark. I widen my eyes in return, mockingly, as though I'm annoyed. But something within me shivers. Some fascination that I've never had the courage to address.

'You're kind of a nerd, aren't you.'

I shrug, heat spilling up my neck.

'I didn't mean it in a bad way.'

'Oh.'

'Thanks for the charger.'

He leaves, and silence settles, damp and heavy.

Jim stopped coming to school, at some point. I tried to broach the subject several times - with my friends, his friends, my parents - but no one seemed particularly surprised. For as much as his life had been loud and unruly; a declaration and affirmation of his existence - his withdrawal from school had been slow. Consistent. A gradual silencing, at which no one batted an eye. I moved on with my life, and he developed into something similar to a myth. Jim Mitchell.

Jodie stumbled to a stop beside me, cheeks bright and eyes glittering with a jarring sort of excitement.

'What?' I half turn, still grabbing books out of my locker.

'Jim Mitchell.'

'Yeah?'

'They found him this morning. In the paddock.'

I face her fully, dread sucking at my stomach.

'Well spit it out, Jodes.'

'Far out, he could've died. He was out all night with a busted pelvis, you know at that turn-off bit? To his road? Anyway, someone driving past early this morning saw him, all minced like that, and called the ambos.'

The dread settled into something cold and painful. Jodie was still talking, all solemn expressions and hand gesturing, but there was a feverish edge to her voice.

'His dad said Jim was out late on his bike, going around checking fences. He told the cops he'd fallen asleep, but I reckon it would've been after a few.'

Jodie exhaled, rubbing at her chest.

'His mum's taking him back to the city, at least till he turns eighteen. Full custody.'

She seemed to notice, finally, that I hadn't spoken yet.

'You alright?

I turned back to my locker, started pulling out books again.

'He hates the city.'

I whisper, and the words clog my throat. Jodie draws me to her.

'I know.'

'He hates his mum.'

'I know.'

Heavier, this time.

'Hey, Mum.'

Yeah?'

'Can you run me to the hospital?'

'Why?'

'Gotta visit a friend.'

We didn't speak on the drive into town. Music from the radio muffled the silence. We pulled into the parking lot, made our way into the waiting room. Settling down into the seat, watching my phone light up with messages, doubt began to pick holes in my resolve. What was I even doing here, really? Jesus, he'd think I was crazy. I looked up, out the window, and saw a group of his friends walking down the sidepath, trying to push each other onto the road. They were like a rude slap of reality, and suddenly my plan seemed laughable. Embarrassing.

'Let's just go, Mum.'

She looked up, confused.

'No way, we're here now.'

'Well, I'm not going in. Let's just go get a cuppa or go home, I dunno.'

Her lips tightened, and I turned my head, shame beating me lower and lower.

'Alright, come on then.'

The car had barely stopped before I swung myself out and headed back down the driveway.

'Jesus, hon, where are you going?' Mum yelled, and I threw the words over my shoulder, tears running down my face and up my nose.

'To the river, I'll be back in one sec, just give me one sec.'

Softness at my neck, the small of my back. The grass pushes up, into me, around me. My fingers dig gentle rivers in the dirt, and small clumps become stuck beneath my fingernails. Spring flirts with the winter still soaking the air, and goosebumps mar the soft skin of my arms and stomach. The light drips through the leaves, pooling on the ground, staining the sky gold.

Years later, and that town wasn't so big anymore. The city held more promise than I knew what to do with; I blew away most of it, before settling down with a half-finished degree in agricultural law. It took a while for me to realise that I couldn't stand the constant noise that ran the sidewalk outside my bedroom window, the tepid cold cramped with diesel smoke. That the tiny town surrounded by dead grass and broken fence lines was the only place that truly set me alight.

Unsettled, I tap the steering wheel nervously. I roll past the turnoff to Mitchell's Road, and my gaze slips from the bitumen to that small mound of grass cradled by barbed wire. My breath catches in my throat as I see him as he was years ago, sprawled on that mound, propped up by his backpack; and me staring out the bus window, committing it all to memory. A four-wheeler trundles past, and I realise I've slowed almost to a stop. The man on it raises his beer to me in blessing, flicking his cap back to expose his sweaty brow. And I feel my face crumple, at that familiar, pointy grin. We sit there like that for a minute, staring at each other. Then he widens his eyes, enough so that I mark it, even from the road. The ghost of a smile plays on my mouth, and I ease my foot onto the pedal.

The Sense Of Endings

Kristof Mikes-Liu

Sandrine. The last day.

The Calamity is nigh. I can sense it. I reckon everyone can, but mostly people shut it out like it is an interruption to the distraction at hand. For all its bad press, doom scrolling is preferable to doom. I get it. It is just that I am not comforted by it. The idea that we might slip not just unsuspectingly but completely obliviously into non-existence terrifies me. It is not that I have some legacy that must be handed down. Legacy would be obsolete anyway. I could be the most downtrodden, unproductive human being on the planet, and I think it would still bother me. The idea, not only of me but of everyone, not being. Boom. Gone. Not tidily closed off by an exclamation mark or a question mark or even a plain full stop. Just no longer. No threads that emerge after the event, no comedy or tragedy, no little nidus of life beginning anew. I call it The Calamity, because of how I feel about it now. When it happens, there will be no feeling about it. It will just be, or have been and be no longer.

*

The other day, I tried to tell my son about it. He is the one most precious part of living for me. I told him everything would end. He asked me if I was having a dig at his driving. He asked me what videos I had been watching on my phone. I told him I had gone off my phone because time was too precious. He scoffed.

'People your age,' he said, 'they get sucked in by scams all the time because they have no media literacy.' How could he know what makes me tick? He ignored the fact that I had few friends my age exactly because they got caught up in conspiracies. They would complain about how things are and forget that our generation is responsible for the conditions of today. The good ones of my generation, mostly, are already dead.

I let him scoff and kept quiet. I noticed the urge to grab my phone and search its cracked screen for *Disrespectful adult sons* or *Why children scoff at their parents*, but I am practised in letting *urges pass*. We shared a nice enough lunch but inside I felt sad. I thought about how he would no longer be. I thought about how whatever it was that made us we would also no longer be. Scoffing sons and affronted mothers would not be a thing. Feeling sad and other human reactions would cease to be.

I tried to think about how none of this would matter after The Calamity. That made me feel more impotent.

*

Maybe I should not fight the end. Maybe I should just let it happen when it happens. When it is done, nothing will matter. Everything, and nothing, will be equal.

Just letting it happen is hard, though. Not holding onto the trivialities that make my being in the world something that exists saddens me. It will not matter that my secret ingredient in ragu is ginger, or that I know that Sofia and Jessamine had a thing while their spouses were away having a separate thing, or that I love single petal roses. It will not matter that my son thinks I am going batty or that I love him with all my heart, or that even though he denies it to himself, as an adult he still blames me for his father leaving. I do not want to let go of what will no longer be.

I have no choice.

The Calamity is nigh and because of this fact, I choose to go for a walk to the shops. I do not take the bus, because I want to walk the path I remember.

The road flanking the mosaic of front lawns and crooked footpaths and sloping driveways.

The turning left and going around and up the hill, passing five blocks until I get to an intersection and crossing it diagonally so that I arrive at the back of the Chinese restaurant on the corner, where they still sell short soup and long soup.

I marvel that once upon a time, someone actually contemplated this area, and made a map that turned into the place I walk through. How did they decide that this would be a block, and that would be a street, and Smith Street would cross Burroughs Street and Finnian's Close and Webb Lane before yielding to the five ways? I have known this neighbourhood for decades. I smile at how it changes constantly in little ways even with the fixed allocation of space. The people in the houses are different from before, the way they occupy each bit of space is different day to day.

The magnificent flame trees in the front of the house on the corner greet me. They were there long before the newlyweds decided to buy the house. Each year the trees declared the end of winter's cold and the arrival of another year of summer's heat. This year, a buddha statue sits patiently between them. Whoever planted the trees is long forgotten, but their annual legacy of a frenzy of red and a harvest of sinister seed pods make me gasp with surprise. Every year, I tell myself that I should have no cause for surprise because the seasons are predictable. Still, the flame trees speak to me as though I had never heard their voice before.

I think about other things that surprise me, even though I know of their existence. At home, I pass the storage room that used to be my son's old bedroom and the past rushes into the present. I remember him as a toddler, a child, a teenager. I think about him now, creating his own life. He is each version of himself. I think about the way he answers the phone with 'Prontola' when I call him because it was our in-joke when he was young. The greeting has survived many evolutions of the telephone. It is less funny than it used to be, more habit than humour now. It is a strange thing to pass down from generation to another.

These things, and so much more will not matter. Being sad about their loss will not matter. The idea of things mattering or not will not exist. From the point of view of now, that is an awful thing to consider even though it will not matter and it will not exist then, when the The Calamity is upon us.

I get to the shops and pass by the Chinese restaurant. It is not yet open but I can see them setting things up and making dumplings inside. I pop into the aquarium and buy a goldfish on a whim. There are many more fancy fish to behold but I overlook them because I know goldfish are hardy and I forget that hardiness will neither matter nor exist. It reminds me of an orange pebble waddling in the water. I decide its name is Cumquat. I stop at The Double Shot for a flat white and a biscuit which, upon reflection, I revise to a Vienna coffee with a slice of lemon meringue pie. (I take comfort in the fact that at some point, whatever I choose to consume will not matter or exist.) The cream is a bit too much but the pie is delightfully tangy and sweet and the surface of the meringue just that extra bit more sticky. I thank Julie and when I pay cash I leave a tip. I pop over to the general store and buy a loaf of bread – multigrain, and a small milk. I survey the store's interior and the hundreds of items it contains and think about how I am familiar with some of the items and may never sample others. It occurs to me that I may not get through an entire loaf.

And I walk home. Chinese restaurant, five ways, Lane, Close, Street and Street. I walk fast to the front door because I am starting to feel like I have to do a wee and wonder if I will reach the loo before my existence is wiped.

I get my wee in.

I start to notice the intensity while I am washing my hands. My body starts to feel quite hot. I would normally call it uncomfortable except I am prepared for this and I want to savour whatever I can sense. After a while, I can no longer distinguish hot from cold. My vision starts to go blurry even though my glasses are fixed firmly on my nose. Everything is brighter which is hard to make sense of because my bathroom does not have a window to the outside, and the light bulb itself does not seem to be faulty. Maybe my eyes are changing. I hear a neighbour scream and some sort of crash outside and all of a sudden all the dogs in the neighbourhood are barking and even some of the cats are mewling so loud it is possible to hear them from within a closed-off bathroom. I think to myself, *Why are they choosing to panic at this moment? It will stop them from savouring what's left.* And I think about my son. I try to keep my last thought about him, even though I know that after it passes, the thought will not matter because it will not exist.

I notice an inbreath. I release a breath. I picture my baby.

*

Sandrine. Some days before.

I am on the bus returning from the big shops. The small shops are closer but limited in selection. They have things that you might want from time to time but not everything you need on a weekly basis. My shopping cart is almost full and was hard to lift from the footpath. I did my ordinary shopping as well as get some special purchases. I have the special mince from the butcher, fresh ricotta from the Greek delicatessen, and a contorted thumb of young ginger. My friends used to ask me about the ginger. *What did I buy it for? How did I use it?* In their opinion, garlic and basil are always enough. I have my reasons, but they are mine to know. Besides, I do not have that many friends anymore. Some have stopped talking to me. Some have moved out of the city, or to higher level care facilities. Some have left the world for good.

The bus arrives outside my house. I am lucky that way. There is a young mother also getting off at my stop. First, she takes the pram off the bus then she helps me with my shopping cart. It is a red shopping cart. 'That's very kind of you,' I say to her. She smiles at me. She seems polite but I get a sense that she has not understood my words. 'Your baby is beautiful. What is her name?' I continue. The situation does not change. She keeps on smiling and then pushes the pram along after a final nod, and smile, and wave. I wave back.

When I get to the kitchen, I remember why I went to the big shops. I will prepare something simple. He is coming for dinner today. Justin. Jason. Jonathan. How can a mother forget the name of her own son? Sometimes it happens, in short bursts. I forget. And then I remember, like it was never forgotten.

Jay. Like the bird, he is beautiful and proud and precious. Like the letter of the alphabet too, straight with a curvy underbelly. (I am not supposed to know about that.) I knew his father, for god's sake and I know something of myself. He may be, he is his own person, but he is also the offspring of two people who knew nothing about how to raise a child and were still figuring themselves out. I sometimes wonder what it was that I wanted back then – probably a friend who I could talk with about anything, who would reassure me and possibly even rescue me. That was a tall ask of an infant.

I stack the fridge and the pantry but leave out the ingredients for lasagne. Everyone has room for lasagne. Almost literally, I can make it with my eyes closed. (A long time ago, I tried, literally, and had to go to hospital to get my finger stitched up. Ah, the folly of young womanhood.)

The afternoon passes like a blur. It is curious how the afternoon light fades slowly and quickly at the same time. I am in the kitchen and the radio is on. That man on the radio is obnoxious, but I have the habit of listening to him. The lasagne is in the oven and the timer is on and I am cleaning up after myself. Jay calls me on my phone.

'Prontola!' I say, a little too giggly for the occasion.

'Mum,' he says. 'That joke is a little tired now.' I say nothing and he continues, 'I'm just ringing to say I'll be a little late – probably twenty more minutes.'

I tell him, 'No worries,' and end the call. It is not too bad. The lasagne will be done and I can keep it warm in the oven. Twenty minutes will not dry it out.

I am setting the table when the thought of not having those twenty minutes with my child pops up in my head. It catches me by surprise, like a thief in the night when you are up unexpectedly because you have a craving for milk and cookies. I have waited twenty minutes for my child before, and more than that. Thirty minutes. An hour. Half a day. Weeks. Months when he had his gap year. Waiting is a part of life. I know that. But suddenly, at this time, I am aware that each particular moment of the twenty minutes passing will never be repeated, and will never be shared with Jay.

'Sandrine, you are overthinking it!' I say to myself, aloud this time. Saying it helps a little, reminds me that this is only twenty minutes and not months. The niggle does not go away. I remember not remembering Jay's name and that brings back the bad feeling. I feel like a bad mother. How can a mother forget her child? I feel like I have no control over the occasions that make up my life.

The bell rings and my worries disappear. It is Jay. He has brought over a bottle of wine and a bottle of chinotto and some sad pastries.

'Save you making dessert,' he says, and I smile. I feel a little sorry for the pastries and then I feel bad that I feel sorry for them. I think about the raspberries I decided not to buy at the big shops. They would have livened up the pastries.

'Thank you darling,' I say. 'Give me those. You take off your shoes and coat and sit down. I'll set the table.' He tells me it smells good, and I think to myself, *Yes, it does smell good.*

It is a simple meal, but his favourite. Our time together is a mix of talking and eating quietly. It is how we have always had dinner together when it is just the two of us. Usually, the rhythm of talking and not talking is comfortable but tonight I fill the not talking parts with worries about losing time. I look at Jay and see how intensely he focuses on chewing when he is not speaking and how he keeps his eyes looking down. He looks up and catches me looking at him and, in the moment, he is partly surprised and partly glaring at me. 'What's up?' he asks, still chewing his food. I lose my balance mentally. I see Jay's father glaring at me through the eyes of his son. The size of their pupils, the small changes toward pink in the colour of their cheeks, the shift of the eyebrows, and the ability to talk through chewing are the same in son as in father. I wince before I remember that now is not then.

'Nothing,' I say. I am still flustered. 'I was just thinking.' He continues to look at me, two men but mostly my son and not his father. I do not notice him blink. 'I was just thinking about how busy we all are and where the time goes.'

'You're a philosopher now?' he replies and for a moment I cannot tell which man it is that is speaking to me. I feel like I have to come up with a clever answer to hide my confusion. I have no clever answers and so I stay quiet. Jay looks at me a moment more and looks back down to his food. I am stuck in this moment even though he has moved on. I cannot move my head or the direction of my gaze. I try to focus on my breath, but I cannot hear myself breathing. Jay raises his head again, chewing another mouthful. His gaze is softer. Maybe he can see that I am stuck. 'It's okay mum,' he says. 'I didn't mean to put you on the spot.' The softness in his voice and eyes releases me and I can move my body again. I can hear my breathing again, although the need to attend to it has passed. I go back to my food, not so much because I am hungry but so that I have something to do. Jay continues, 'The lasagne is delicious, it really is.' His words are an offering of peace. I accept peace.

'Thanks son,' I say. 'I know it's your favourite.'

We eat for a while.

As he has his last bite, the feeling of worry comes back to me. I think about the moments I wasted staring at him without the ability to speak. I think about how soon he will get up and head home to Sharni and the kids. The clock will start again, counting down the time to the next time we see each other. I try to tell myself that he has a life outside of his relationship with me and that it is the passage of time as much as the amount of time together that brings people closer. My own arguments do not persuade me.

His plate is clean and mine has a few mouthfuls of lasagne left. A tear runs down my cheek and eventually drops onto the dinner plate. I look at him again. Justin, Jordan, Jimmy. His name escapes me again. The feelings inside me expand but I cannot put the right words to them. 'You'll be out of here again before I know it,' I say. My comment upsets him.

He rubs his eyes. I can tell that he is trying not to let his frustration get the better of him. I am pushing him away and holding onto him at the same time. The more he tries to control his feelings, the more intensely I look at him. He scoffs. 'Mum, you're doing it again. Why can't we just have a meal without it becoming some high stakes hostage negotiation?' I want to be invisible but all I am is mute. I can feel more tears drip down my cheek onto my food. They make the pasta look like it is sweating. 'That's enough. I have to go,' he says. He gets up and puts on his shoes and grabs his bag and walks at faster than normal pace to the front door. 'Thanks for dinner,' he half-mumbles.

The door is closed. He has left his coat on the arm of the sofa.

I cannot make sense of what has happened, of how we keep on getting into this dance of trying to have a nice time and failing. I get up out of my chair and collect the plates on the table and bring them to the kitchen. I put the pile of dirty dishes next to the outpost of stale pastries still encased in flimsy plastic.

I feel bad.

I try to call Jay to tell him that his coat is still here, but the call goes to message. I do not have the strength to craft a message so I hang up. I throw the phone across the room and regret my lack of diplomacy as well as the damage done to the phone. The feeling of time escaping comes back in a wave that is more intense than the one that has just passed. Instead of feeling tearful, I notice the urge to wail and bawl my eyes out. I compress all of that feeling and force it into a final, single tear. Perhaps, I am losing my mind.

I leave the dishes and sit down beside the coat on the sofa. I notice the strangest sensation. It is hard to describe, harder than trying to remember your own son's name when his name escapes you.

I think of a garden patch that is suddenly covered in shade. At first, the gardener assumes that a cloud is overhead, but the shadow remains and grows bigger and bigger in size. All of a sudden, the gardener realises that it is not a shadow but the absence of the sun that is affecting his garden patch. This is not a temporary problem, but a forever problem. As the gardener figures all of this out, he also realises that if the sun is no longer, then it must be more than his garden patch that is affected. If the sun is no longer, then nothing can be the same as it was. In that moment, the gardener ceases to be.

I think about being both the storyteller and the gardener. I think about the tale of the gardener and the garden patch as though it could be a single moment. If I could capture what that single moment feels like, I could go some way to describing the strange sensation that flows over me. I wonder if I am losing my mind, becoming more frail, maybe feeble.

I try to tell myself that I have felt this sensation at different points in my life. The harder I try to convince myself, the less I believe my own thoughts. It would be easier to think I was losing my mind. The alternative is that I am experiencing something real in the world, something I have much less control over.

The feeling refuses to settle. It wreaks havoc with my insides, the insides of my thoughts as well as of my body. I feel panicky and breathless and sick. I worry about my son, about how he has a life before him that this feeling threatens to cut short. I try to bargain with the universe and trade never seeing him again for him having a future to navigate. It feels like flinging prayers into a vast and unamused emptiness of space. Every thought I have tightens around my chest and points to the fate of the gardener. This sensation feels dreadful and callous, also complete. It portends disaster. It is calamitous.

It is The Calamity.

Both my cheeks are dry of tears.

✶

Jay. Some weeks before.

I just veered off the road. It wasn't a big drama. I mean, it cost me, but in the end, no harm was done. I didn't have to take any time off. I didn't get much sleep because they insisted on me being cleared in Emergency. It took a while, but that was it. I power slept in the spare room after getting home and was right as rain to get to work the next day. I reckon I got as much sleep as I usually do only it was condensed into five continuous hours rather than eight interrupted.

Sharni wasn't that flustered once she knew I was okay. 'The insurance will cover what's left,' she said on the phone. Heart monitors in other cubicles and overhead announcements marked time's passing. The next day was going to be a busy one for Sharni, with school drop offs and booked appointments. Plus, her seminar was three days away. People lapped up her advice on Unlocking Individual Success, probably because she took nothing for granted. I thought to myself, *She'll probably use tonight as a learning point for the seminar, share a real life lesson about how distraction can literally result in you veering off your path.* I admired how capable she was in staying focused. I wished I could execute my duties with her clarity and ease. We met at one of her seminars, long ago, and I haven't attended another since.

Mum, on the other hand, freaked out. *Why didn't I call her? What took away my attention? Did I swerve to dodge a kangaroo?* I mean really, a kangaroo in the Inner West? She'd been fretting, unable to get hold of me on either phone. Eventually she called Sharni and got the low down (and I imagine, a touch of the old cold shoulder – mothers- and daughters-in-law). The annoying thing was that she need not have found out. If she had read my text from earlier that day to say I was cancelling our usual catch-up for dinner, she'd've been none the wiser. She told me her phone was playing up which made no sense because I saw that she had received and read my message. I sometimes wonder if she isn't losing it a little bit, forgetting stuff, misreading situations, getting into arguments with old friends. Once she got the salt and the caster sugar mixed up and we had to settle for take-away dinner. She hasn't figured out how the world works in this day and age, and the situation's getting worse.

She wouldn't have understood why I had the accident. It was silly, really, like a slapstick comedy. Sure, I was a bit tired. The day had been long, but we were close to deadline and there were a couple of reports I had to pull together. More than a couple, but nothing I couldn't achieve. When I veered off the road, I was thinking about the design and formatting of the cover, listening to some podcast about the bushfires, picking hot chips from my lap, and trying to find my phone. Smart phones love to play hide and seek, and they're good at it. You try to grab them and they bounce away and find the most niggly of hiding spots. Driving nowadays is an exercise in multitasking. I know I'm not the only one who does it. I just got a little unlucky.

It didn't kill me. If anything was going to kill me, not meeting the deadline would've. It's literally in the word: deadline.

Sharni made me visit Mum the next day. 'I can't deal with your mother's texts right now. I have to focus on my presentation.' I guess it would make up for the cancelled dinner anyway, though I had to skip lunch to get through my task list.

Mum had roasted a chicken. I told her day-old lasagne would be fine but she insisted that it was inedible, and full of the fated night's bad luck. Whatever. We sat and ate. Out of the blue, she started talking about the long summer days of her childhood and how she would spend hours wandering through the woods.

'What's this got to do with anything?' I asked.

'I was just thinking about how you're so busy you don't get to appreciate what you have.' That comment riled me, like she was blaming me for having to work hard.

'Mum, you don't understand. This is how things are nowadays.' She went quiet and I could tell she was trying to hold back from saying something else. I tried to cut her some slack. I started to think about how her earlier life might have been different to mine, but I stopped. I knew I'd end up feeling guilty and guilt interferes with success.

We stayed silent for a while, chewing food. 'Do you have room for dessert?' she asked, eventually. 'And maybe an espresso for the road?' She didn't usually offer me coffee at night, so it wasn't hard to figure out that she was trying to make sure I got home awake. I rolled my eyes.

'You know, a small accident isn't the end of the world! You don't have to turn it into a drama.' I was frustrated by her interference. It was just a small accident.

She got up and took the dishes to the kitchen and got the dessert out of the fridge. I could hear the coffee grinder grinding. The whirring sound reminded me of the feeling I get at the bottom of my ribs when I feel stuck; and my thoughts go round and round without getting anywhere. I looked for a distraction, and the placemat before me caught my eye, with its scene of a café by night. It looked like Paris and the opposite of feeling trapped. I had the thought of dropping my guard.

Then I thought about how I was an adult and not a child, and I pulled myself together. 'That's a No to the coffee, Mum,' I shouted into the kitchen. It felt weird to say those words. The whole sequence was strange. Like the chain of events that led up to my prang. What if I had crashed into oncoming traffic, or into a wall? Where would I be then?

I knew she was going to make the espresso anyway and I was going to drink it anyway. I had the strangest feeling that the world was going to end. But not today.

Wife in Silhouette

Kamille Roach

It was not a chance encounter.

The gentleman at the back of the room rose from his seat as she entered through the glass door of the busy Fremantle café. His white hair was a beacon in the gloom, and she could see his teeth because he was smiling. She noticed his shirt.

She remembered it was one of his many blue work ones from years ago. Even now, it looked good with his blue eyes.

As she got closer, the healthy flush in his cheeks delighted her. She walked over to him quickly.

He wrapped her in his powerful arms, tightening them as if to communicate vitality. 'Didn't think you'd come.' He kissed her cheek. 'I'm so glad you did.'

She returned the greeting, which brought his mouth corner warmly close. They stilled for a moment. 'I've missed you,' she whispered.

With her heart so near to his, she could feel his blood pulsing.

Her body responded, feeling sturdy with turgidity like the leaf of a succulent. Substantial.

She tightened her grip on him. 'Where else would I be?'

She held John for as long as she could, but not long enough to be noticed by anyone around them.

An awareness of the surrounding crowd made it seem suddenly louder.

She eased back, face tilted upwards. 'Should we order right away?'

She noticed him swallow.

His smile was brief. 'Sure, but it will have to be decaf.' He made a face. 'Have you ever heard of anything so ridiculous?'

She laughed silently with her mouth open.

He blinked twice, touched her arm and indicated a table. 'I'll order.'

'You remember mine?' she said.

He shook his head as though it was silly for her to ask.

Once they were seated across from one another, she reached out and took his hand in both of hers. 'How do I look?'

'Young. Ready for anything. I envy you.' He chuckled, but his smile faded quickly.

She squeezed his hand. 'You can't be alone today. This is the most brutal part.'

He swallowed hard, and his head moved as though he were watching someone cross the room behind her.

She waited. In the past few days, she found that patience, jealousy, and sadness were no longer an issue. She tried thinking about emotional situations involving John, someone new, or the children getting hurt, but she felt nothing.

'The funeral was a week ago,' he said, voice breaking.

'Exactly. That's when everyone goes away- '

He lifted his hand for silence and closed his eyes.

'Look at me,' she said. 'I feel better when you do.' She glanced around, but no one seemed to notice them. 'We're not doing anything wrong.'

He sighed, reopened his eyes, and smiled. It was the smile he'd always kept just for her. As though she were his favourite person in the entire world. A little warmth brushed her skin, and she imagined she could feel the temperature of the day.

Fremantle was hot, not that she could feel it. She could tell by the glare of the sun and the sweat patch on people's backs and beneath their arms. The road and footpath can get so hot even near the sea, so everyone, even the homeless, had to wear shoes or risk burning their feet.

'I have a plan,' she said.

He nodded slightly. 'I knew you'd know what to do. I'm lost- '

'Shhh.' She held a finger to her lips.

She looked down at her thighs. They were covered in a translucent peach cotton skirt. For a moment she remembered how the muscles in her legs had felt as a child before running races at school carnivals, and later as an adult, riding horses.

Concentrating hard, she channelled John's heart rhythm, his warmth and strength. After a moment, her pulse began a slow, weak rhythm. A tingling sensation came from her limbs and chest and she could imagine her cells and fibres awakening from their cool, sleeping state. Then she noticed her weight against the wooden seat. Despite her grin, John appeared slightly distracted by the staff activity.

Next to them, a repetitive, propulsive grinding came from the coffee machine. She inhaled deeply but could not smell it.

John flinched, his eyes fixing on the big, black square making the noise. In the small serving area, staff were swiftly taking orders and jotting them down, then placing tickets on the bench. The barista glanced at the orders, both hands busy on the machine levers. A waitress dipped and opened a glass cabinet. Inside was a cheesecake, raspberry slice, and savoury muffins.

She lowered her voice. 'John, I'll come home with you.'

John cast a low glance around. 'Really?'

The ideas came quickly then, and she felt her body take more shape in anticipation. She pulled back her shoulders, using almost forgotten muscles, and enjoyed the sensation.

'You need sleep. Or maybe a movie, something kind to the mood. I can keep myself busy reading emails… or something.' Her certainty wavered. No one would wait for her replies. Her inbox, if John hadn't cancelled it, would be full of advertising from businesses she couldn't remember subscribing to.

She locked her eyes on John's. 'You said I look young? I don't want to be too young.'

He blinked. 'It's like…you've had the boys.' He saw her wince and went on quickly. 'But they're grown and gone. They're okay.' He dropped his eyes and was still for a moment.

She touched the back of his hand. He didn't respond.

She concentrated on the crown of his head and drew air deep into her lungs, the sensation like cold water inside her throat. She remembered for a moment how good it was to gulp down lemonade on a hot summer's day.

'Is the house free?' she said.

It usually was, but these days, time was a slinky thing that slipped back and forth. At least she remembered how long ago the funeral had been. She'd been the centre of attention, after all. But she only got that right because the date was on a dinky wooden calendar on the counter beside them. It had numbered cubes that could be rotated to display the date and month each day.

John lifted his gaze. 'Yes,' he whispered. 'Come home with me?'

She felt the weight of her arms and then the length of her legs, the feature John had said he'd first noticed. She ran her hands down her thighs. 'Shouldn't we wait for the coffee?' she looked around. 'They'll notice if we just leave.'

'I didn't order any.' He shrugged slightly and his cheeks drooped. 'Decaf.'

She walked through the doors into the sunshine, the pastel cotton fabric of her skirt brushing her calves. For a moment, she disappeared in the brightness and wasn't sure where she was.

Walking behind her, John remembered her in that dress. He'd called it her peach dress, and they'd then tried making a drink by blending canned peaches, vodka, lemon juice, and a little sugar. Their kisses had been sticky, which had made her giggle.

John looked back and waved to the barista. The young man was frowning as he moved between the machine and the bench. 'Flat white with one! Soy latte! Two long blacks!' he said over his shoulder. He caught sight of John and his eyebrows flickered up in acknowledgement.

John walked out and drove home alone.

She was there waiting by the front door in the shade, a shoulder casually wedged against the wall near the entrance bell. The dusty string moved in the wind. John inserted the key into the lock, and together they walked into the gloom.

'Which movie?' he asked.

She frowned slightly and walked into the lounge, cradling her elbows. 'Does it matter? Maybe we should just play music. I think I'll sit with you until you go off to sleep.' She turned to face him and watched a few expressions cross his face. 'It's okay. I'll be here when you wake. If you want me.'

'Want you?' he inhaled deeply. 'God, I can't describe how much I want you. It's all the time, an ache.' He covered his eyes with his hand. 'I've been turned inside out.' Even in such pain, John radiated a soft, warm glow. She imagined his soul bright as the sun.

She put her arms around him. 'I'm sorry. Thank you.'

She felt more confident, his need filling her with ideas, possibilities. She could even fell her thighs were warm against each other. Could they go to bed together she wondered?

John walked over to the kitchen bench and quickly straightened a pile of papers. He glanced up. 'I've been told that seeing you here is natural.' He frowned. 'According to my counsellor, it will stop at some point.'

She pointed for the bedroom. 'Please have a rest. I'll sit with my hand on your chest, so you know I'm there. You look exhausted.'

'Not too tired.' He gave her a look.

They lay side by side, naked. She didn't remember the undressing. This happened sometimes. A slip forwards, a skip back, like she'd slept when she blinked.

He ran the back of his fingers from her shoulder down to the crease inside her elbow. The sensation felt like a cotton sheet had moved across her. He leaned closer and kissed the side of her neck.

Kissing John had been one of her favourite things when she was alive. His lips were soft, and he was gentle at the right time, and more vigorous when she needed him to be. Never had another lover felt as in sync with her as John.

She closed her eyes. Then it was easy. Their intimacy was a dance of slow harmony built from years of knowing where and how much. She hadn't known she could bear his full weight until he lay on top of her. Then another pleasant surprise. She felt him inside her. Felt him as if she were alive.

Afterwards, he held her tight. She felt the strange buzz of his fear, felt it mingle with hers, creating a wavering mirage which gave her a seasick sensation.

She watched his chest rise and fall for a while and then pulled the covers up and put her arm across him to keep warm. He breathed deep and steady. She matched his breaths as though oxygen was something she needed.

Alone with her thoughts, she wondered if this was bad for him. She decided it was not. During their marriage, sex calmed them both and brought them closer than conversation. Making love had dissolved tension and made talking possible.

John slept for half an hour. When he woke, he checked his watch and noticed she was still there. He smiled widely.

John got to his elbow, hand supporting his head. 'When you woke, you were always light hungry. You said it made you feel properly alive.'

'I know, but…' She indicated the heavy dresser and mirror blocking the window, which was also covered by a blue curtain. 'I also liked the privacy.'

The public footpath was just outside their fence.

John sat up. 'Let's move that across and open the curtains so when you wake up in the morning, you can see out.' He got up but stopped with his legs hanging over the side. After a moment, his shoulders heaved. She heard him sniffling.

Quickly, she jumped up and began pushing at the dresser.

Wiping his face, John looked over. Briskly, he joined her, rubbing his chest with the heel of his hand. 'Here, don't do that by yourself!'

Together, they wrestled the furniture to the side of the window.

She stood in front of the curtains. The light didn't quite reach her as if she were a shadow and light simply fell around, creating her silhouette.

'You're so beautiful,' said John.

'Please don't cry.'

He looked away.

She cleared her throat. 'We're going to clean that grubby window,' she said determinedly. 'Then we'll shower and go out.' As he protested, she stopped him with one hand. 'Let's take that little walk around Fremantle like we used to. Then we'll have the ten-dollar burger.' She grinned.

John's face lit up, and he grabbed her around the waist and wrestled her into his chest. For a moment, it felt real.

The walk, the burger, the unexpected live band which comprised two men who sang Moon River and Coward of the County, was perfect, John said. His mood seemed lifted as he put an arm around her waist.

She held his hand against her stomach. 'I love being here with you.'

He slowed and then turned so that they were facing one another. 'When…do you go?' he asked.

She looped her arms over his wide shoulders and their bodies drew close. They pressed into the familiar embrace. Passing car's headlights and taillights swept past along the narrow road, illuminating John but never reaching her.

When you let me go.

She couldn't say it out loud. Because he'd think that's what she really wanted. But that was the opposite of the truth. She was selfish, and he was kind. It had always been this way.

She pressed her lips against his, and then they walked along hand in hand.

She remembered when they met. It had been a bright Saturday morning at the Fremantle markets near the donuts stand. After they'd walked around for a couple of hours, he'd taken her home. She remembered fondly that she hadn't left for two days and two nights.

She missed her university classes while he went to work the following Monday. Upon returning home, he found her freshly showered and waiting in his bed after she had cleaned his house. She easily recalled his face shining when he'd seen her there.

John's housemate's rapid exit followed the agreement she should move in. As the housemate left, handing her the keys, he winked. 'Be good to Johnno. He has a soft heart.'

John's soft heart had held a few more secrets, which they later found out with a cardiologist, bleeping monitors and surgery to install a pacemaker. Because of that and the fact he was older than her, she'd always thought John would die first.

After they'd arrived home from the pub, they made love again. John didn't fall asleep right away. He got up and stood in front of the window, naked.

The skin across his back and buttocks caught her attention as it no longer appeared stretched taut, but had wrinkles resembling soft ripples in folded linen. It was as though his skin had finally relaxed around him. Since retirement, he'd had room for quiet mornings drinking tea in bed or sitting outside with his feet up on a chair.

'In the morning, I'll get started in the garden,' he mumbled.

Sometime later, when she wandered into the garden, the sun was high. She was unsure if she'd slept in John's bed or if it was the day after or more time had passed.

She noticed John by the fence with a shovel and wheelbarrow.

As John scraped moss off the pavers with the shovel, his face filled with purpose. He stopped for a moment and rubbed his chest.

'Would you like a cuppa?' she said. John shook his head but smiled softly to himself.

'Let's get two chairs and a little table for out here,' she said, raising her voice. He lifted his eyes and scanned the veranda before he gave a nod.

'I'll get them when I go to the hardware store. I'll need supplies for the pond,' he said.

'Oh!' she covered her mouth.

John grinned. 'Told you I'd get round to it.'

John made two trips to the hardware store and then took three days to install the pond. He stopped regularly, sitting on the edge of the veranda to catch his breath. Once it was complete, he looked everything over with a satisfied expression.

'It looks amazing,' she said.

He smiled. After a while, he got up slowly and walked away.

She followed him inside. 'John?'

'I'm tired,' he said thickly.

They held each other close, but John's arms were loose. He soon began to snore.

She felt John fade.

As she grew cold, she concentrated on the pond and garden and imagined how they would sit together out there with a cold glass of Gin and Tonic. They would welcome the grandchildren back for a visit, plan a barbeque. The house would be full of noise and action like it once was when their sons were small.

It was another afternoon when she got back to John. She floated between the pond completion and now, struggling to recognize familiar places in Fremantle.

John didn't know this was where she went when he didn't need her, this sort of unfocussed, foggy limbo. There but not there. Somewhere in between.

She found him on the floor of the lounge room. He was on his side, one arm bent awkwardly beneath him.

Cheek to carpet, he had his mouth open.

'John?'

She'd known it was coming. It had to happen, but it was still shocking. She squatted down and held her wrist in front of his mouth. Warm breath slowly came and went. She tried to push him onto his back, but her arms felt thinner and weaker than ever. She looked around, threw her hands up in the air, and then rushed over to the bench.

A small slip of paper caught her eye. It was a form, like the one the

GP wrote when he ordered a blood test. But this was a different colour. This one was from the cardiologist.

She touched the form. It moved slightly, and it took her several attempts to get a hold of it. She walked outside and went to the neighbour's front door.

She tried but couldn't move the string which was attached to the gong of the doorbell. She closed her hand into a fist. Her knock was silent. She growled, but a passing truck swallowed the sound. Somewhere a dog was barking. Then she heard the far-off whoop of a siren.

She wondered if John would need an ambulance. Could she bear to see him taken into the big white building where she might lose him? Shouldn't they be together? She knew that's what he wanted. It was why he kept thinking about her, wishing her back so hard that she hadn't been able to leave.

He needed her.

She raced back to John. His skin had a greyish tinge. She got down on the floor and carefully lay her body along his. She kissed his cheek, seeking the last of his body warmth. Her lips came away tacky.

It felt wrong to wait like this. Stand by as he faded. Watch his light die.

She got up and raced next door.

This time, she could ring the doorbell. The door opened. A stocky man filled the doorway. Wearing loose track pants, he rubbed his eyes with one hand, yawned and winced in the sunshine like a creature after hibernation.

She opened her mouth but couldn't make a sound. Instead, she focussed her energy on the man's big, heavy body and imagined moving him in John's direction. Like a solid brick wall, he wouldn't budge.

The man looked left to right. She waved her hand in front of his face.

The man suddenly frowned at the ground. He held the doorframe as he sank into a squat.

She saw him pick something up. It was the Cardiology form. She must have dropped it.

The man glanced sideways towards John's open door. Despite his size, he moved quickly as he walked over and disappeared inside.

'Are you alright Mate? Oh shit. Calley!' he called. 'We need an ambulance!'

Wearing a multi-coloured dress, a woman ran past.

John's wife watched Calley disappear inside her old house.

She remembered it must have been a year ago that she'd walked out into the moonlight - a faded woman in a white nightdress, after she'd received her diagnosis.

End stage liver cancer. The beginning of her disintegration had begun, pain and then pain killers. She'd felt herself fade through the weeks until she was nothing. Finally, all of them had hugged her and then let her go, leaving the room empty except for John. He had sat beside the bed crying onto the back of her hand for a long time.

From the corner of the room, peace had beckoned her like a warm whisper, but the sight of John had stopped her following it.

John didn't want her to go. He wanted to be with her. He wanted to die.

The siren was loud, but noise and heat and discomfort were no longer a concern. She watched as two men in uniform stretchered John out to the ambulance. It sped off like a bee with its sting on fire.

Something brushed her hand. John stood strong and tall beside her. His eyes were on the gap the ambulance had left.

'How does this work?' he asked.

She squeezed his hand, but it had no more weight than hers. Not like it had when he'd been alive. His face turned, and he smiled, his blue eyes the blue of the reflected sky on a window with space behind it.

'I'm not sure. I was only here when you needed me. Between times…' she shrugged.

'We're together now.' He grinned, taking her other hand. It felt cool and feather light. 'We can make love all day long if we like.' He gave a short laugh.

She forced a smile, knowing it wouldn't be the same now.

She looked away. 'I should have got someone sooner instead of trying to keep you to myself. You were always the good one. Look at you.

Even dead, you glow slightly.'

It was true. John emitted a weak light as if some sunlight was caught inside him.

'Don't be silly.' He took her in his arms, but it was as light as being wrapped in a lace curtain. She wanted to feel the crush of his chest against hers.

'I'm where I want to be,' he said. 'With you.'

They kissed. She supposed they kissed. His lips felt as substantial as air. John sighed and told her it was just like it always had been. But he wouldn't meet her eyes.

She let him lie. He'd always been the kind one.

'I only wish…' John looked off toward the departed emergency vehicle. He remembered the two men alternately pushing on his chest and squeezing a bag of air into a mask over his mouth. Hopeless activity, the duty to provide life-sustaining measures to a recently widowed old man with a heart condition.

'What?' she said. She could still hear the siren. If they had given up hope, they surely would have turned it off.

'That the grandkids could see the pond,' said John. He clicked his tongue.

Suddenly she understood.

'Go! You have to…stay. For them.' She turned him around and gave him a shove, which drained every cell of her being. It was only enough to set him forwards one step.

Then something happened. Light swept through her and it felt endlessly bright. 'I'm letting you go, John,' she said. 'I love you!' But she was talking without sound and there was no one to hear.

John was gone. She looked up at the sky and inhaled the sun-drenched air and felt something soft and peaceful. She drifted up towards it.

In an ambulance crossing the Old Fremantle Bridge, a machine stopped its flatline drone of death and began a hesitant beeping. Once, twice, then a rush of regular bleeps which indicated a heartbeat. Inside John, a tired old artery opened a little, and some blood flowed. A paramedic smiled with surprise, called to the driver, and increased the flow of oxygen. The ambulance mounted a curb to evade a blocked intersection and sped towards Fremantle hospital.

'John!' said the paramedic. 'Hang in there, buddy. You're going to make it.'

Mouse in Paris

Jodie Kewley

It feels surreal - me, here, in Paris. It's nothing like I pictured, not this part of the city, anyway. Sure, the buildings are old but there's graffiti and cigarette butts everywhere and a hot gritty wind making things seem shabby. Still, as the taxi pulls away, I can't help feeling jubilant. I've made it, alone, abroad as Dad would have said.

The apartment is on the second floor. Its door is slightly ajar. I push it a little further, hoping I'm in the right building. 'Fiona?'

'Mouse, is that you?'

At the sound of my sister's voice, at the name no one else has called me, I forget that for years I have hated her.

'I'm in the lounge room, Mouse. To your right.'

I follow her voice into a room where piles of books lie on the floor and clothes stiffen on a clotheshorse beside closed French doors. Fiona is on the couch, her plastered leg resting on the edge of it, crutches propped up against the wall near her head. Her face is thinner, her brown hair - cut short now – is curly. She has her arms out. There are tears, hers and mine.

'I can't believe you came all this way!'

Fiona smells of cigarettes. 'I can't believe it either.'

'Gosh,' she says when she has let me go. 'Look at you, a grown woman.'

'A tired woman.' I don't need to look at a mirror to know that my clothes and hair are crushed from the long flight, my eyes small and pinkish.

'But you're here.'

There's a fan on in the corner, its air lifting up the edge of a newspaper pinned down by an upturned milk crate. Empty coffee mugs and a bowl with remnants of cereal are strewn beside it. All these years I'd envisaged Fiona living somewhere chic.

'We should celebrate,' says Fiona. 'Have a look in the fridge, I think there's a bottle of white. There could be some bubbly.'

There isn't a kitchen as such, just a sink, an oven and a fridge at the other end of the room, with a long wooden table separating the two areas.

"There used to be a bench,' says Fiona. 'It used to look like a kitchen. I used to have bookshelves, nice ones Lucien built himself, but then when he left, he took them, didn't he? Hence the mess.'

She says it without rancor, as though she's accustomed to men letting her down. When she'd mentioned Lucien's desertion in an email, I'd thought that she might be heart-broken. I guess I don't know her very well.

The fridge is full to bursting, a fair proportion of it alcoholic. The very first bottle I pull from its depths appears to be champagne.

I hold it up for her to see. 'There's this.'

'Perfect,' she says, and laughs at me wrestling to get the cork off. 'You'd think it was a dangerous animal.'

Truth is, I'm not much of a drinker, could count on one hand the number of times I've had a drink before three in the afternoon. But today it seems entirely appropriate.

We make a series of toasts - to sisterhood and stronger bones, to Paris and us – until our glasses are empty and I feel slightly vertiginous. There is so much to talk about, so many years that need to be colored in that I don't know where to start, and I find myself talking about the ice storm that hit Melbourne on my way to the airport and the boy with Tourette's on the plane. I'm nervous, I realize, over-excited.

We've started on the second drink when Fiona gathers up her crutches and asks me if I'll open the French doors. There's a chair on the tiny balcony facing the street where she must go to sit and smoke. Next to it is a dead plant in a pot, its soil studded with butts. There's hardly enough room for the two of us, with me standing and her crutches.

She makes a half-hearted apology before lighting up. 'But, you know, almost everyone smokes here.'

I lean against the railing. It's still hot but there's a smattering of rain. Someone closes a window in the apartment opposite. Immediately below us a girl on a scooter plaits her way between pedestrians. Something about her triggers a memory.

'Remember the time Dad found those cigarettes in your bag?'

'No,' says Fiona. 'What happened?'

'You know, you'd been out, you must have come home late, and you were wearing make-up, which he hated. And then he found the cigarettes. He was furious. He made me get up. Then he made you stand in front of the mirror – you can't have forgotten that - and smoke, in front of me and him. He wanted you to see what you looked like when you did it. I guess he did it to stop me from taking it up too.'

'And?'

'Well, you took a big drag, like an old movie-star, and blew it out, with him behind you saying not so pretty now, are we, young lady? Then you leant forward and kissed your own reflection. Left a big red lipstick mark.'

Fiona gives a hoot of laughter. 'No, really?'

I'd never thought of it as anything but a painful memory, a precursor to her leaving, but now I find myself laughing too.

'Imagine what he would think if he could see us now,' I say, 'drinking champagne at this time of day.'

'He's dead, Mouse. Who cares what he'd think?'

*

It's a one-bedroom apartment. Fiona offers to sleep on the couch but she's better off in her own bed near the bathroom. Besides, I like the idea of moonlight sliding in through the lounge room's French doors. While Fiona's cleaning her teeth, I send a quick text to Alison, Arrived safely. Thanks for the lift to the airport. Say thanks to your parents for the neck-cushion. M x. It is all I can manage. Then I help Fiona to bed, fatigue rolling over me like a breaker.

'Thanks again for coming, Mouse,' she says. 'You're an angel.'

'Sleep well,' she calls from her room.

'Don't worry,' I call back, 'I will.'

But at some point I wake, thinking I'm at home, and I listen hard, wondering if Dad has called out or fallen or both. I can hear my heart beating so hard it hurts. Everything in me has tightened. The darkness, the silence, seems loaded with danger.

Then the noise recurs, a snore. Fiona is snoring. And I remember that Dad will never call or fall or both again.

*

It's so light when I open my eyes I think it must be late and I get up quickly, guiltily. But it's only six-ten. I pull open the French doors and stand there, breathing in the warm foreign air of the city which Dad liked to claim had seduced him when he was a young man. The city, he declared, that had captured his soul, before he'd met my mother, before we were born, when he, it seemed, was a different person, one we would never meet.

It's cloudy. The wind has dropped. There's no one in the street, just parked cars and a single black dog, nose down, zigzagging along. I'd have some breakfast but I don't want to wake up Fiona, so I prowl around the lounge room instead, looking at her books and at the photos on the fridge and the mantelpiece. Fiona's in most of them. It's clear she has lots of friends, male and female, and that she likes to party. She doesn't shrink from the camera the way I do. There are lots of her god-daughter Genevieve and a couple of me, one taken at my graduation, the other of Paul and me when we started going out. There's one of Mum holding up her first attempt at pottery, a misshapen bowl. And another of Mum with me on her knee, Fiona standing at her side. I hold it up for a closer look.

'You're up early.'

I have the ridiculous urge to drop the photo I'm holding, as if I've been caught doing something I shouldn't.

'Oh sorry, didn't mean to give you a fright.' Fiona drags herself to where I'm standing.

'I was just looking . . .'

'That must have been taken just before she died. Her hair had started growing back. She was pleased about that. We used to run our hands through it, remember?'

I don't. I don't remember anything about her, no matter how many times I go through the albums at home. And yet sometimes I feel she is there just beyond my peripheral vision, that if I turn around quickly enough . . .

'I don't remember having seen this photo,' I tell Fiona.

'That's because I took it with me.'

'Oh.'

Her leaving home hangs in the air like a whiff of smoke.

*

I thought we'd spend the morning together talking, but Fiona insists that I go out, see the sights. Besides, she says, she has work to do and she hunkers down on the couch with her laptop. Navigating alone through the streets I feel both conspicuous and anonymous. I wish Paul was with me. He'd have loved Paris. He knew about architecture. With his lean frame and dark hair, his slightly effeminate air, he would have fitted in. I can still recall the look of surprise on his face when I told him I had a sister.

'No way! How come you've never mentioned her before?'

I'd shrugged. 'She lives in France.'

'You've got a sister in France and you forgot to mention that?

'I haven't seen her for years. She left when I was ten.'

We'd been walking to the uni café, but he stopped and said, 'Your dad hasn't mentioned her either. What am I missing here? Did she do something wrong?'

It was cold and windy and I didn't want to be having this conversation, especially not outside, but he wasn't going to budge.

'I don't know. I guess she did. She and Dad used to be really close but then she hit puberty and they fought like cat and dog. She left when she was sixteen. She pretty much ran away.'

'Ran a long way away.'

I gripped his arm. 'Paul, don't say anything, will you, to Dad.'

'Why not?'

How could I explain that Fiona had become like a wound in what was left of our family? 'Because it broke his heart, her leaving like that.'

*

I don't venture very far from Fiona's apartment. I'm not ready to visit museums. Everything still seems slightly unreal. I stop at a small square and sit on a bench opposite a café where a girl in a short skirt sets up tables and chairs with sulky efficiency, her ponytail swishing. A man wearing a black apron, leans against the café doorway, smoking. He says something to her, then flicks his cigarette out into the street and disappears inside. An old woman, hugging a bag of shopping, sits on one of the other benches, and fans herself. Blurry through clouds, the sun emits a weary kind of heat.

I find myself wondering if Dad ever sat where I am sitting, and wishing I'd paid more attention to what he'd said about his time here – where exactly he'd stayed, which bar he'd frequented, because he had definitely talked about a bar, a bar with flock wallpaper and a pianola. He'd talked about a girl too, some girl from the south of France – Veronique or Violet, something starting with V, at any rate. I want to believe that, having shed his body, he has become omniscient, can see me from above and understands that part of the reason I'm here is because of him.

Even now I want his approval.

My mobile pings. It's Alison: So, what's she like???

It was Paul who tracked Fiona down. It wasn't hard. Having edited a number of left-wing magazines, she had quite an online presence. He said I should write to her, and I did, a short, tentative, rather formal email. It felt like a subversive act. She wrote back that very same day, suggesting I come to Paris, as though there was nothing to it, as if Dad with his stiffness and tremors could be left to manage alone.

I text Alison back, Nice, then delete it. Great. I delete that too. Interesting. That doesn't seem right either, but I leave it, adding, All good. Talk soon. Promise X, knowing she'll be disappointed. She and I have been friends ever since I can remember, but when Fiona left we became closer still. I tell her everything. She'd offered to come with me, even though her own father, Abe, is recovering from a serious stroke. Uncle Abe, I call him. Uncle Abe who swam in the sea every morning of his life no matter what the weather, who gave up sugar well before That Sugar Film came out, who bought Auntie Evelyn a Jack Russell terrier pup for their 40th wedding anniversary to encourage her to exercise. It still doesn't seem fair.

When it is all set up, I shift to one of the café's outside tables and order coffee. I try out some of the phrases I've learnt at my French classes on the ponytailed waitress, but she instantly reverts to English. There are more people out and about now; people who smoke while they walk, people with dogs, children with satchels on their backs who must start school later than in Australia. Sparrows scamper around near my feet like mice. I can't remember the last time I sat doing nothing, even on the plane I was busy doing French grammar exercises. I stay on even after the waitress has slipped the bill under my empty cup.

*

'What did you get up to?' Fiona asks when I get back. She's in the same position on the couch, computer resting on her stomach.

'Not a lot. I had a good time, though. I bought some bread and cheese for lunch,' I say, offloading them on the bench. 'I got a paper too, The

New York Times, which I thought you might like to read. Oh, and this.' I hold up the postcard for her to see - Les jardins de Luxembourg en automne.

She smiles. 'Another place you've got to go to. Who's it for?'

'Uncle Abe and Auntie . . .'

'Abe?'

'You know, Alison's parents.'

'I know who they are,' she says. 'I just didn't realise they were still hanging around.'

I'd forgotten how dismissive she could be about some people - so like Dad in that way.

'They were very good to us,' I remind her curtly, 'after Mum died, and all through Dad's illness and when you . . . you disappeared.'

She starts typing and says, without looking up, 'I didn't disappear.'

Two weeks in Paris suddenly seems like a long time.

*

She apologises, in a fashion, over lunch. 'Deadlines,' she says, 'I always feel ambushed by them, and this bloody leg. I wanted to be able to show you round, but . . .'

I tell her not to worry, that I don't mind exploring on my own.

'Which reminds me,' she says, 'whatever happened to Paul?'

'He met someone else.' I'm surprised at how steady my voice is. I can't bring myself to tell her that he's already engaged to her and that I can't forgive him for that. 'I don't think either of us expected Dad to take so long to die.'

'Shame,' she says, and I don't know whether she means that's a shame or shame on him or shame Dad took so long to die.

I allow a space for her to ask about Dad - his life, his death, his funeral. I want to tell her that I have brought with me some of Dad's ashes to scatter, perhaps in the grounds of the Sorbonne where he studied so many years ago now, and that I thought we might scatter them together. I want to ask her if the reason she came to Paris is because Dad always talked about it with such reverence. But she drags herself up and propels herself awkwardly to the balcony. Cigarette time.

*

The afternoon passes quietly. Fiona works and takes calls and smokes. I take a nap (on Fiona's bed) and clean out the fridge and read through my guidebook, taking notes. Just when I'm thinking about what we'll have for dinner, Fiona tells me that friends are coming over.

'For dinner?' There's no hiding my dismay. Despite the nap I'm ludicrously tired and I still hoped that tonight we would reconnect, Fiona and me.

'Don't worry. They'll all bring food. You'll love them, seriously. And they're all dying to meet you. They all have to work in the morning, so it won't be a late night.'

She's right, they do bring food, as well as grog, but so late I'm almost post-hunger. And they do seem pleased to meet me. They ask what my first impressions of Paris are and how long I plan to stay. They find physical similarities between Fiona and me that I can't see. Their English is better than my French. But as the night wears on they talk between themselves with an ever-increasing volume of hilarity and vehemence. I'm pretty sure they are writers or performers of some sort or another and most of them seem keen to impress Fiona. After a while, I give up trying to understand the conversation and focus on appearing to look alert when in reality I'm flagging. I can't stop ruing the fact that I can't go to bed until they leave. Fiona, on the other hand, is as alive as I've ever seen her. Her teeth are tinged purple from the burgundy and she's slurring a little but she's smiling, laughing. She doesn't know what it's like to be shy.

The last one, Guillaume, leaves after midnight, kissing Fiona smack bang on the mouth, even though he's clearly gay.

Although her friends have made an effort to clean up, the dishes haven't been done; they're piled up in and around the sink. Fiona's still sitting at the table, picking at a cheese platter.

'Hey, just leave them,' says Fiona, when I pull on gloves and turn on the hot tap.

But I can't bear the idea of waking up to them. 'Has to be done some time.'

'Yes, tomorrow. Genevieve's coming over tomorrow. She can help.'

Why on earth should your god-daughter have to do them, I think, when she wasn't even here for dinner? But what I say is, 'No, I'd rather just get them done now.'

'God, such a martyr. So passive aggressive.'

The pipes judder loudly when I turn off the water. I turn to face her. 'I think maybe you've had too much to drink.'

'Yeah? Well, maybe you haven't had enough, because maybe if you had you'd just come out and say what's on your mind. Look, I know you're angry that I didn't come back but, you know, you didn't have to look after him, Mouse. You could have found somewhere for him to go. A nursing home or a . . . whatever they're called.'

'You think I didn't try? He wouldn't have it, Fiona. You may as well shoot me now, is what he'd say whenever I tried to bring it up. You don't know what he was like,' I say, forgetting for an instant that he was her father too.

'I do, actually.'

I pull off the gloves slowly, try to collect myself. 'Is that why you left?'

'I didn't choose to leave exactly.'

'What does that mean?'

She downs the rest of the wine in her glass. 'I was pregnant, Mouse. That's why I left. When Dad found out he was – well, you can imagine - outraged. He wanted to know who the father was because he wanted to kill him. I mean, I don't think he meant it literally, but I think he was expecting some young punk he could drag up by the collar and wave his fist in their face.'

'So who was it?'

'Abe.'

'Abe? Not Uncle Abe? Are you serious?'

'It's not what you think, Mouse.'

'Abe?'

'Okay, so he was a lot older than me, but I loved him and I thought he loved me too. He told me he did. He told me again and again. But then when Dad found out about the pregnancy, Abe denied it, didn't he? And who did Dad believe? Yeah, that's right, his best buddy. He gave me a thousand bucks and told me to 'get rid of it'.

'Uncle Abe did that?'

'No, Dad did.'

'Oh God.'

'So I caught a plane to Thailand, spent some time at a backpackers, met a French guy, followed him here, and the rest is history.'

'Fiona, that's just awful. Why didn't you tell me?'

'Apart from the fact that Dad wouldn't let me? You were such good friends with Alison, I couldn't. I'm sorry. I just couldn't.'

'No, I'm sorry. '

The tap drips behind us.

'You know what?' says Fiona, seizing her crutches, 'I need to go to bed.'

It takes me a moment to find motion but then I follow her to make sure she doesn't fall. I help her out of her clothes and into bed. She opens her arms, the way she did when I first arrived. We hug briefly, wordlessly, without leaving time for tears. She says nigh-nigh like a child. Her eyes are already shut before I switch off her bedside lamp. I, on the other hand, don't feel tired anymore.

'Fiona?' I ask before leaving the room. 'The French guy, was he with you when you . . . when you had the termination?'

'I didn't have a termination,' she murmurs. 'I had the baby. I had Genevieve. Can we talk about this in the morning?'

I go back into the main room and pace around, blowing out the candles and picking up crunched-up paper serviettes that have been left on the table and the chairs, then I have a proper look at the photos of Genevieve that are scattered about and wonder how I couldn't have realised that she was Fiona's daughter when it was staring me in the face. There are so many photos of her – as a baby, in school uniform, on a ferry, on a stage playing the violin, at a graduation ceremony. And when I examine them more closely, I can see that she has our mother's broad, open face and Fiona's chin. There is even something of me in the way she holds herself, or so I like to think.

I do the dishes, wipe down the sink, carry the rubbish downstairs all the while recalibrating the past, the present, the future.

Fiona snores.

*

The first birds are starting up when I carry the vial of Dad's ashes on to the balcony and shake them on the pot plant. I feel I should say a prayer, something about his soul having been set free, about peace and forgiveness, but I can't think of one. I make myself a cup of tea and sit at the long wooden table with the postcard I bought for Uncle Abe and Auntie Evelyn. It looks so peaceful, the image; a large pond with orange leaves floating on it, the sky and trees reflecting off the water. I turn it over and sit thinking for a moment, then I start to write quickly, before I can change my mind,

Dear Paul, here I am in Paris staying with Fiona. I'm so glad I came. You'd love it here. You should come with Sophie one day. Congratulations on your engagement. Guess what? I am an aunt! M x

Ticking

Justine Sless

Dave's in his Y- fronts, so, there's no way he's going to get up and push her into the waiting taxi. He's sat up in bed and he's going to stay right there, because y fronts have a sneaky habit of being a bit too baggy, and if there's any jostling to do, a testicle is quite likely to pop out.

A nice quiet morning it was, 'til Pam walked into his room, carrying a load of black bin liners, like she was going to do a tidy up, but bold as brass, had stood at the doorway and told him that she was courting Bobby Johnson.

'You what?' Dave had fairly spluttered his tea across the room. 'Bobby bloody Johnson? You've got to be joking.'

Pam had shaken her head, twiddling her charm bracelet, the bin liners rustling like a musical score.

Dave thought he'd noticed something different about her. 'How long?'

'Three months.' She'd whispered back.

'Well pet, it's him or us. That's all there is to it.' Dave shook his newspaper out, assuming that was that and Pam would go into her room, listen to one of her records and come out later to say sorry. But no, she'd taken in upon herself, and no doubt Vera was in on this as well, and she'd said;

'Him.' like she was choosing gravy, rather than a splash of vinegar on her chips. 'Mam's called a taxi.'

That caused Dave to cough up a hoick of phlegm into his crumpled cotton handkerchief and he'd not even lit up his first ciggy of the day. When the heaving in his chest slowed down, he'd folded his newspaper up slowly, taking in this person standing there, interrupting his Sunday morning. It's all a man wants after a hard week's work; a lie-in on a Sunday morning, the newspaper, a cup of tea, proper milky with two sugars.

'Vera! He commanded her to come upstairs to do some explaining. Calling a bloody taxi. All he'd done for these two over the years, fed and clothed Pam when her own father had waltzed off into the sunset with God knows who and to God knows where.

'Well, you can get out, I'll not have filth like you living here. And you can leave that record player, don't think you're taking that with you. Leave it right where it is, cost good money that did.'

There's the toot of a car horn.

'Vera! tell that taxi to stop making a racket, we don't want the whole street knowing our business.'

Why a taxi has been called is beyond Dave, there's the bus stop at the end of the road. Dave's pleased he'll not be paying for the taxi. He blames Vera really; she's always been too soft on Pam. Calling a taxi. Pam will go off with that Bobby Johnson and Vera will be snivelling and trying to get her back home. But he won't be made a fool of, not in his own house. There's no way his good name will be dragged through the mire on account of Pam's poor choices. He's got his reputation on the darts team to maintain. That kind of respect is hard won, and he's not about to lose it now because Pam has gone and got herself mixed up with that filthy lout.

Him or us. Reasonable and fair. She's 19 as well, old enough to know better.

Dave had left home by the time he was 16. But Pam, she had an education, finished sixth form, on his bloody watch. The newspaper needs to be read, Sunderland's lost again, he wants the details of the disgrace, and his tea has gone cold.

'Vera! Make me another brew.' Dave taps out a Woodbine from the packet. Whorls of smoke billow from the shield of his newspaper, ending the conversation and leaving Pam no option but to go to her room and start packing.

*

Vera's pacing in the kitchen, as if the linoleum isn't worn enough. She's not even had a cuppa, probably wouldn't be able to keep it down anyway.

She'd seen Pam and Bobby kanoodling in town on Friday morning. Pam was looking up at Bobby like he was a prince and Bobby was all cat's got the cream looking at Pam.

A pimply lad from school would have been better than this, anything would have really.

Vera had a quiet word with Pamela on Friday night. 'I know you're seeing him, he's no good, best end it.' Pam had denied it at first.

Then in a voice Vera didn't recognise and with a look of pure scorn, Pam had just shrugged and said,

'So what?'

Now it was Sunday morning and Vera was in bits. She'd tried pleading with Pam.

'It's Bobby Bloody Johnson, he's had more women than you've had hot dinners love, think about that.' Vera didn't tell Pam that she'd pashed him back in the day. I mean really who hadn't? He'd try it on with anyone.

'But I love him, Mam.' Pam's voice a childish whine.

'Don't be soft, Pet. End it now and there'll be no more said.' Pam, her eyes downcast, had sighed, 'But..'

'Oh, Pet you're not up the duff are you?' Vera's mind was racing with where to call and get rid of it.

'No, I'm not having his baby.' Pam's biting her bottom lip.

'What then? End it Pet, we needn't say a word to anyone, especially not to him.' Vera's head tilted in the direction of the stairs.

Pam had shaken her head. 'I can't.'

'Then you'll have to take your things and leave' Vera hoping the finality of the word leave would shake Pam out of her stupidity, but Pam had crouched down to the kitchen sink cupboard and torn off four black bin bags.

When she'd stood up, she'd sneered at Vera and said, 'This is true love, this is.'

'True love eh? Go upstairs and tell him about true love. I'll call a taxi.' The word taxi taking Vera closer to a blubbering mess.

As Pam walks upstairs to tell Dave, Vera riffles through the phone book for the number of a taxi. She'd never called one in her life, but this situation called for a quick exit. Pam had money from working in the arcade, and Vera certainly wasn't going to pay for the embarrassment of it.

Vera stood stunned when the woman said, 'Where to?' Pam was already halfway up the stairs.

'Pam, where are you going?' She'd hissed, Pam frowned back at her.

'To tell Dave.'

'Where does *he* live?' Vera's voice a tremulous whisper.

'43 Worcester Terrace.' Pam ascended three steps closer to telling Dave.

Worcester Terrace, a row of old houses converted into bed sits. She'll not know what's hit her living there.

When she hangs up, Vera isn't sure who she feels sorrier for; Pam going to Bobby's bedsit, or her being left alone in the house with Dave.

*

Pam stares at the rows of books and teddy bears in her bedroom. She hugs Big Ted and smells his fusty familiarity. She wants to take him but is afraid that Bobby will laugh at her for bringing it. She looks at all her ornaments, as familiar as Top 40 songs. The bulge of the black bags dictates her decision. She takes a small ceramic kitten and her black bound notebook, filled with poems and doodles of hearts whole and broken.

She shoves in clothes, two pairs of shoes, some records and her prized pink and blue striped jeans, they'd cost a whole week's pay from the arcade, where she'd been working since she left school. She felt like a queen when she'd walked into Ku Club wearing them that Saturday night. She'd seen a man leaning against the bar, leather jacket, tattoos, smirking at her. He'd done this nod, a beckoning of sorts. She'd sashayed over, they didn't say a word. He'd leaned towards her, thrust his tongue in her mouth, the smell of beer and cigarettes on him, the pressure of his hand on the small of her back, enthralling.

She takes her round timber clock from the bedroom wall. There is a white cut out cloud on one side and the arch of a rainbow on the other side. As she pushes the clock into a bag, her finger catches on one of the thin brass hands, it snaps and the clock stops ticking at. She nearly weeps then, at the shock of it all, but knows that now is not the time for soul searching. She tips out her savings from her Holly Hobby money box into her purse and takes one last look around the room.

She expects Dave to be out of bed, the spidery hairs over his pale chest showing beneath his limp brown dressing gown. She is hoping for a kind word and a tenner to help her on her way. But he's sat up in bed. His face is twisted, and he is hurling insults at her, each one of them as punishing as the next. Pam pulls the unwieldy shapes of the black bags closer to her and stumbles down the stairs.

Vera is at the front door, their eyes lock briefly. The street is a ripple of twitching curtains.

A burly taxi driver opens the boot of the car. He doesn't comment or help Pam, as if he senses the shame of the situation and doesn't want to be sullied by it. Pam heaves the bags into the jaw-like boot of the car. Her cat Biggles stares at her from his spot on the windowsill as they drive off.

Her breathing is heavy for a moment at the thought of leaving her cat behind, but as they turn away from the street, she feels a surge of excitement at the thought of all the sex her and Bobby will have. They could lounge around for hours afterwards; she could even cook them egg and chips for their dinners.

Pam sits up straight to take in the view from a car, everything looks a bit different than it does being on a bus. There's a show of autumnal splendour in Backhouse Park. She cannot place the emotion, but her skin feels heavy and uncomfortable at the memory of her knickers twisting and her back bruising against the bark of the huge oak tree in the park, three months ago. The sound of Bobby's grunting, the feeling of him thrusting into her, turning all the imaginings she had ever had of losing her virginity, into a reality.

The taxi rounds the corner to Worcester Terrace. Pam jumps out and says, 'Wait here.'

The taxi driver glowers at her.

'Have to keep the meter ticking, time is money.' His right arm hangs over the edge of the window, his fingers drumming a tattoo of irritation.

Pam wishes she was arriving with a fancy suitcase rather than misshapen black bin liners, but the truth of the matter is that her, Dave, and Vera had never been on a holiday, so there was no need for suitcases.

The front door is off the latch, it always is, because of the constant comings and goings. Pam bounds up the stairs, her skin an explosion of excitement. On the first landing there is a waft of burnt toast and baked beans, the shared sink a wreck of washed and unwashed dishes.

The bathroom door on the second landing is open, the window is fogged and the floor awash with puddles of water and a greying scrunched-up bathmat.

She hasn't seen Bobby since Friday; they'd had sex quickly in the lane way on the way back from the pub. Bobby's groaning had made her excited and anxious in equal measure.

Pam is out of breath by the time she reaches the top landing. She brushes down her jeans and pulls her parker on straight, imagining

Bobby lying naked in bed, thinking of her. Pam wants this moment to be special, but the taxi was already up to three pounds and twenty pence and she won't get paid again still Saturday. She has no idea how much living with Bobby will cost and the thought momentarily disarms her. She knocks, knowing that Bobby's embrace will fortify her.

When Bobby opens the door, his face is a mask of thunderous scorn, not unlike Dave's, Pam thinks fleetingly.

'You've done what? Left home. Fuck.'

Pam inclines her head, willing him to kiss her. A kiss will unscramble it all.

'I've got my stuff in a taxi, I thought you could give me a hand to carry it up.' Her words withering into a whisper.

'Jesus Pam, you can't live here.'

'Who is it babe?' A woman's voice queries.

Heat bolts though Pam's body and lands with a red flush on her face.

'You'd better go home, Pet.' Bobby's voice lowers. His hands flutter briefly like he might just reach out to her, but when the question from inside his bedsit is repeated, he shrugs and wordlessly and closes the door.

Pam makes her way down the three flights of stairs, the light on each landing cutting through the grime.

'Thought this was the drop off point.' The taxi driver slams the boot shut. 'Where to then?'

The only other place Pam can think to go to is the arcade. Debbie will be there, opening for the day. They'd been friends for a while now, stacking up piles of pennies for customers to spill into the machines, arranging prizes that were rarely won and scoffing hot chips together at lunch time.

Debbie knew about Bobby, 'Careful' was all Debbie had said.

The meter is up to six pounds twenty as Roker beach comes into view, the sea is flint grey, and Pam is wearier than she's ever been.

The taxi driver takes her money and slams the boot shut. He hesitates before he gets back in.

'Planning on sleeping here then?'

Pam is so focused on keeping her possessions together that she doesn't answer.

Debbie, her smile as brassy as her bottle blond hair, takes in all of Pam's bags and asks matter-of-factly.

'Bobby?' Pam nods.

'Let me get the kettle on, then I'll come and give you a hand to get this lot inside.'

Pam turns towards the sea, it is uncharacteristically calm today, small waves folding over themselves and arriving at the shore in stripes of white foam. A gull hovers over the camber of the pier and a lone walker, heads towards the red and white striped lighthouse.

Anthem

Alida Galati

September's arrival always signifies two things. Hay fever and dancing. The hay fever seemed to be getting worse with ageing, but, thankfully, was easily managed with a daily antihistamine. As for the dancing—or the time travel, as she affectionately refers to it—one particular song never fails to transport her to her early teens and Saturday afternoons at the roller rink. Skating around and around, forwards, backwards, fast, slow, crossovers … In step and gliding with the rhythm of the music. The DJ always playing the best of the Top 40 hits.

Of meeting Rob.

*

She'd first seen him at the rink with his mates at the tail end of summer and into the early weeks of autumn. She didn't think they looked the type to be interested in skating, and yet, there they were. They all looked the same, dressed in their weekend uniforms of faded blue jeans and checked flannel shirts, unbuttoned, over the top of white T-shirts.

But he'd stood out. Over those Saturdays she observed from afar. She liked the look of him and his easy manner. The way he laughed with his friends and mucked about on the rink, all the while skating confidently to the music. He looked like fun. Her friends could see the crush that was growing and gently teased her about it. She felt herself blush every time they said something. It's not that it wasn't true – but it was never going to happen. As she repeatedly pointed out to them: We haven't even looked at each other at the same time, let alone spoken!

Then, he disappeared, as did all those boys. Rumour was that they played footy for the team the next suburb over, so Saturdays at the rink were now impossible. Out of sight, out of mind, she and her friends simply went about their business of skating. Secretly though, she did think of him, more than just occasionally.

Those Saturday afternoons were glorious times for her and her friends. They'd all known each other since primary school, but now they went to a mix of different high schools so seeing each other was virtually impossible during week days. The roller rink was their place. Being allowed to stay most of the afternoon, listening to music, skating and catching up on all the news (ahem, gossip) at their respective schools, and the people they knew in common. There was nothing like it. It was, without a doubt, the highlight of the week for them all.

A few months later—and to her utter delight—those boys, including him, returned.

Oooh, look who's back?! said her friends. She turned to look at the entrance and saw that group of boys walking towards them, skates in hand, but then stopping at the booths closest to the snack bar. She sought him out—couldn't miss him—he'd grown taller, was taller than all of his friends. He was skinnier too, but even from where she was standing she could see that same open, friendly-looking face. Noticing that he had looked in her direction, she blushed to her roots—her friends laughed—and escaped the attention by pushing off from the side of the rink, and skated, focusing on nothing but the middle distance and the beat of the music.

It was the first weekend of September. She'd never forget it.

That was the start. Something had shifted in those boys and over the course of that spring, they casually managed to merge with her friends, so that within a few weekends, they knew each other's names, were chatting together and all sharing the same couple of booths when taking skating breaks or leaning proprietarily at the same space on the far wall, near the DJ.

That DJ. He was upbeat and energetic and loved nothing more than to draw attention to the skaters and getting them onto the rink. He loved a full rink skate-dancing to his tunes. He happily took requests and even played party games to get everyone involved. He paired people up. How embarassing!, she and her friends would exclaim. He even played the occasional slow song 'for all the lovers out there', announcing it using his corniest American accent.

One time, he ran a 'dance off' skating game, playing his favourite disco tracks. All her friends, and those boys, joined in—free icy poles all afternoon were on offer—who wouldn't want to win!

Over four songs he eliminated the skaters not up to scratch, and left the ten remaining on the rink for the final, fifth song that would determine the winner. To make it fair, he said, he'd play a brand new single that had only just been released a couple of days earlier so that no-one had had any listening advantage. All the skaters pushed off. This dance beat was fresh, unlike anything they'd heard before, the rhythm of the bass easy to move with, the lyrics were catchy — and it was impossible to skate without a smile on your face.

(Later, as her musical knowledge grew, she would learn that that song wasn't just disco, but a blend, a fusion, of funk and R&B.)

She was one of those top ten still skating, as was Rob, and they both were absorbed into those three and a half minutes of melody and movement. Often skating past each other, toward each other, competitively trying to outdo each other — all the while grinning, with full eye contact.

Over the previous few Saturdays they'd chatted quite a few times—talking about school, homework, records, TV and movies—and though she'd felt giddy thinking about those conversations later at home, at the time they'd always felt comfortable and normal. Real.

But that song, that music—and that moment in time—was the catapult. Their connection magnetised. Their friendship grew … and then, over time, more, and more. And it was the most natural thing in the world.

*

Now, decades later, sighing and rubbing her aching hip, she's acutely aware that she's no longer that young girl, and that each passing year brings with it a new limitation (or two). The physical ageing she feels is one thing, but the physical changing of things around her is what continues to surprise—sometimes frustrate—but always amaze her. She doesn't need birthdays to trigger this self-awareness: this month, every year, does it without fail.

This is the first September without Rob.

With him around, the small light-hearted ritual at this time of year was fun — even if it did seem silly or childish to keep harking back to the past. But their long, shared history had made it worth doing. It brought a smile to their faces, everytime, every year. Rob would tease her about the 'Spring Time Travel Anthem' but he always joined in, laughed and sang, sharing the happy, nostalgic skating dance with her — sans skates, on solid ground. She's still close with a couple of those school friends from the days at the roller rink and even they would laugh at the quirky ritual after all these years — but, with a touch of envy. Some relationships, they would reflect, were just meant to be.

Their children too, now grown, with partners and families of their own, recognised, and even admired the importance of this romantic tradition. Ironic really, as they'd spent their childhoods totally embarassed by those public displays of affection.

Somehow, the song never aged, as they physically had. Or maybe it was just their perception and what it meant to them — especially to her. They marvelled at the changes its format had undergone over the years. Just like them, once youthful, now moving beyond middle age, its metamorphosis too, was unbelievable. Astounding. Vinyl, cassette, CD, an iPod download, streamed on the computer, and even the phone. But the song, its essence, remained.

*

Today, with lots of time on her hands, and feeling the nostalgic pull for the sound of vinyl, she goes downstairs to the rumpus room. She hasn't been down there since the end of last summer when they'd had the pest controllers come and deal with a cockroach infestation in the kitchenette. She shudders just thinking about that, and it's now with trepidation that she opens the door, turns on the lights and enters, hoping there are no creepy-crawly surprises.

Looking around she finds herself catching her breath. At Rob. The space is just as he left it when he was last down here. The old carpet, the worn couch, the TV, the sound-system, the record and CD collections, the overflowing bookshelves. His spare glasses on the coffee table, on top of the weekend newspaper … of that wretched Saturday.

Her eyes start to water … she blinks quickly—two, three, four times—stopping the flow.

His beloved, worn footy scarf on the armchair comes into view … she breathes in deeply— holds it—and slowly exhales.

She goes to it, picks it up and she can smell him. Wrapping it around her neck, and hanging down her torso, she feels him, right there with her.

Walking over to the turntable she sees there's still a record on it, its cover on top of the speaker. 'Australian Crawl.' Stuck in the past, she chuckles, remembering his favourites. She carefully removes it and places it into its plastic sleeve and then the cover. Moving to the shelves, she knows to file it alphabetically by artist. Her eyes then scan to the right and she stops at E … Earth, Wind & Fire. She pulls out the album she's looking for, and admires the cover artwork. Standing back in front of the stereo, she then takes the record out, and—out of habit—blows on it gently to remove any dust, and places it on the turntable. Switching on the power button, she hears the familiar, faint hum of the speakers come to life, and carefully places the needle on the groove for their song. Side 2, Track 7. September.

Turning the volume to ‘max’—the scarf held tightly, comfortingly, across her chest—they dance.

Trucker Priests of the Nullarbor

PH Court

Shaman, Holy man, businessman, con man, I don't care what you call him. You can even laugh, you won't be the first, just because I wanted to put my faith in a myth. But you can't even begin to know what it's like, to need this healing, to look and never find it.

I've been at the hospital, festered on those sweating plastic chairs while the girlies in their uniforms snigger behind manicured nails and painted cheeks.

'Oh it's nothing, go home you silly man.'

It's not nothing. It's a torment they can't heal.

The shrink was no good.

'It's all in your head'.

'Well bloody well get it out!' I cried. And how I cried. He couldn't remove it from my head. His soft voice and fresh starch. How can he know this terrible itching?

So yes, I tried everything before I took to this road. This long, gloriously open road. No cold benches or cosy waiting rooms. No thumbed magazines and suspicious gazes. Just me, my terrible itching, and this hitching thumb of mine, that has brought me along this ancient road. Well, ancient by Australian standards. For years I sought healing from the very people who, now I see, caused my sickness.

But not out here.

Galahs swirl in twilight storms as the endless night replaces the bottomless day. Out here, beyond the x-rays and lotions, out of the reach of cortisone and prescriptions, here is a deeper reality. Here might I find real healing.

How did I hear about him? Assuming he is more than a myth? I heard of him on my radio. No, not that one. The CB, the old Citizen's Band set my old man left behind when his heart decided he no longer needed to be alive. It had been in the cupboard beneath the stairs. (The radio, not his heart.) I heard it calling to me. Maybe not calling to me, maybe I just knew it was there and felt that it may hold the answer. 'Calling to me' makes me sound like a nut case. I'm not a nut case. I'm a curious case. Perhaps even angry. Nearing the end of my tether, most certainly. Sometimes I wish my heart would opt to end things for me too, get me out of this torment. It is a granite growth inside me. Hard, unyielding, unmoveable. But I'm not mad. The tiny dial glowed green, the numbers telling me of the 42 channels of citizen's bandage that wanted to talk to me. Mostly it said 'hiss.' Just static. Occasional conversations would emerge from the hiss of the little box, like fish rising to the surface to breathe, before subsiding into the murk again.

And then I heard of him. Two men. They spoke in slow, clipped grabs. They had some verbal shorthand that suggested words didn't matter, but what they were saying did. And they mentioned the holy one. Okay, that's not what they called him that first time. 'Yeah?' was what they called him. And 'Y'kiddin?!' But then I heard others speak of this myth, this philosopher, this mystical man of the road. He was out there. He was somewhere in the vast reaches of the hiss and scratch of emerging and submerging voices. The one they spoke of. And he was a healer. That's what they said. A holy man. A miracle man. Out there.

Beyond the houses and towns. Past the everyday. Beyond human habitation. 'Y'Kiddin?!' He was out there, somewhere.

That's why I'm here, beneath the squalling Galahs, as sunlight hurries off to hide from the cold monolith of the looming night. That's why I'm standing here at this outback truck stop. Alone, confused, wondering how on earth dust can have a smell. Do people say 'Stop and smell the rocks'? No. Dust shouldn't have a scent. But it does. Eau de gravel. Perhaps I'll ask the prophet about it. When I find him. The tang of excitement hangs in the air too. A dozen or so slumbering trucks are splayed across the dirt lot, faithful hounds sleeping by the door awaiting their masters' return. And one may well be the one I seek.

This is what I guess you would call the inner sanctum, the holy of holies. A curtain separates the sleeping compartment behind me from the cab.

Rocky had plucked me from the gritted breeze outside the truck stop. He was hauling feed out to Nyabing, near the Fitzgerald River, and now he carried me too. The cabin was warm, dark like a cinema. Expectant. We both stared out at the screen and the golden-blue light lit Rocky's face. He was a small nugget of a man, a beard with a gnome hiding inside it. He had barely grunted as he flawlessly fondled the gear shift through its confusion of mechanical variations until the road hummed monotonously beneath us. The dotted white lines snorted under the nose of the massive truck like bullets and the night loomed before us, a massive tunnel with no light at its end.

'Do you know of this man, the one they call the holy one, the priest?'

The little beard giggled.

'Dunno 'bout no priest but there's a lot of holy men out here.'

'Really?' I urged, excited.

'Oh yeah…'

He paused. The road hummed.

'They is wholly nuts!' A bark erupted from inside the beard. It was a moment before I realized he was laughing.

'Oh. Right. Very funny.'

He looked across at me a moment and the movie of the road reflected in his eyes as sparkles within the facial hair.

'You're one of them eh?' He stared back out through the windscreen and the road hummed again.

Did I really except to find the holy man so easily? Surely not. The quest would be a long and hard one and only the pure of heart would succeed in meeting the great man.

Or something like that. So I sat and waited for the miles to fall away, the snake skin of distance, as I out grew it. There was a grunt from the beard.

'Look, you want the truth?'

I looked at him suspiciously.

'Well, yeah.'

'Hm.' The road hums. 'Look at this. Nothin' but road, night and your own head and whatever you put in it right?'

'You could put the radio on.'

'Nah. Then you get stuff in your head you don't want.'

'Okay.'

'So's anyhow. Out here, everyone gets to be a philosopher if ya want or not see? I mean, you think about it. Who else in the world got time to just sit… and think… just ponder, see?'

I looked at the beard more closely now and I'm sure he was grinning beneath the beard. Or wincing. It's hard to tell really.

Then I understood.

'You are a holy man!'

The beard grunted.

'Nah. Well, maybe.'

In the same old reflected light, he looked different now. The eyes more caring, the beard more a soft down than a bramble.

'And you have gleaned amazing truths?'

Grunt.

The road hummed a while. Rocky took a swig from the water bottle nestled in the console between our seats. He cleared his throat.

'Oright. Yeah. Some things out here, they get to be kind of amazing…'

I turned in the big soft seat to look more directly at Rocky.

'... and you kinda think to you self.'

My heart tripped. A philosopher's tale was about to unfold. This was the beginning of knowledge, the wisdom that could set me free of my terrible condition! My pulse quickened as his crunchy little voice continued.

'About thirty, thirty-five clicks out of Mudamuckla, I was draggin' a load of beef back from Mingenew when I saw there was this lump in the road. First I thought it was a cow or somethin', dead like, lyin' down. It was nearly dark, so I couldn't see real good. I slowed, she was right in the middle of the road...'

His crackly voice was nearly a whisper and sometimes I almost lost his words in the deep thrumming of road and engine. So I listened harder.

'But it was too big, and too, like, pyramid shape, you get me?'

I nodded, open mouthed.

'So I slows right down, I'm in second gear, near enough to stallin' and I pulls alongside this pyramid of, kinda, blackness in the middle of the road see?'

I nod. His voice slows and drops still softer.

'Then I sees the pile is... steaming. Like it's alive.'

The road rumbles. And hums. I stare at him.

Eventually I can't stare anymore.

'What was it?!' I demand eagerly.

With a deep foreboding he utters two words.

''Roo shit.'

I blink and sit back.

'I'm sorry?'

''Roo shit. A massive steaming pyramid of fresh hot 'roo droppin's.' He whispers earnestly.

I stare at him and then turn to face the road.

'You stupid man.'

The beard chuckled.

'You's not listenin' is you? No. See? You come out here seeking the truth and you can't see past the shit. Think about this. A pile of fresh, hot 'roo shit in the middle of a highway… How did it get there?'

Um.

His little voice growled quietly again.

'It got to me see, 'cos I realize the horrible truth.... Out there in the dark, was one massive 'roo, a massive 'roo of incredible size…'

He turned to me.

'… and appetite.'

The truck hauled us through the towering night. Neither of us spoke for some time. He didn't want to. I didn't know what to say.

'So what hap…'

'Ah!' he cut me off. 'It was nearly two hours before the mystery was resolved.'

He chuckled again.

'In me headlights I seen him like a loomin' shadow more'n a creature, like it was only the idea of itself, you know what I mean?'

'Not really,' I admitted.

'Oh. I guess you had to be there. Anyhows, I slows right down again and when I gets closer I see it's just a 'roo, an ordinary 'roo. And he turned his head to look me right in the eye. Just an ordinary 'roo. An old man, a red, sure enough, a big 'un too but nothing like the monster size that could have made that pile of steaming crap. Then he winked at me.'

Rocky snatched a glance at me. Nodded slowly as we thundered headlong toward the west.

'I was stunned! I slowed down even more an' I cruised past this big old red and I noticed the most incredible thing.'

I leaned forward to look deeper into his mystical beard.

'Yes?'

'This kangaroo…' he whispered, 'was completely and totally hollow.'

There was a rumbling, humming silence. I stared at Rocky. He stared at the road. Then he barked and barked, the crackling laughter erupting from deep within his beard.

A few minutes later, when the barking had ended and the little man had wiped his road weary eyes, I chanced a question.

'Is there a point to your story?'

He took a deep breath.

'Yeah. That there is. There's only one way to live.' He nodded gently. 'Don't be full of shit.'

He barked again and for a moment I though he was going to keel over and die like my old man during that football grand final.

'Rocky. You're an idiot'

So here I am by the side of the desert road in the middle of the night watching Rocky's rig become vanishing red spots on the horizon. I'm sure I can still hear the barking laugh. No, now it's just gritty dirt and a coldness near my feet as the desert sheds its warmth and becomes a frigid wasteland.

Bloody hollow kangaroos. Useless.

There is a tiny suggestion of light from the stars but nothing else. Eventually my eyes adjust fully to the silent darkness and still I can see nothing but the hint of broken white lines. I follow them and notice the air here is warmer as heat escapes the black tarmac. Then lightness. Then, golden light, a distant rumble. Again, my heart trips slightly. The trucker priest is out here. I know it, I can feel it. Perhaps this is the light of approaching enlightenment.

It's a Freightliner. Cab over job with a flat front like a cliff made of chrome and lights. A thin, crusty face looks down at me as the following dust and diesel exhaust swirl about me, pulling my hair and scratching at my eyes.

'What da fok you do'in maaaate.'

'I'm trying to hitch a lift.'

'How'd chew got out 'ere?'

'Another guy. He gave me a lift. But I think he was crazy.'

The crepe face raised a wispy eyebrow at me.

'Hah, Probably blooding right too eh?'

'Um… yes. So can I have a lift?'

The thin face scanned the impenetrable dark from beneath crisp bony eyebrows.

'Don' sees why not. Less maybe I is a crazy bloke too eh?'

His sneer unsettled me a bit, but the silent darkness of the empty desert at my back was worse. I clambered up the white wall, like scaling a refrigerator, and hauled myself into the cabin. Music was swirling softly about. Classical, like wildflowers, light and refreshing.

As we roared across the Nullarbor plain I had to tell him about Rocky and the hollow Kangaroo, lest he think I was the crazy one for forsaking a perfectly safe truck cab in favour of the cool hard desert. Julian just nodded occasionally and said 'roight' a couple of times.

'So you's lookin' for truth eh?'

'Yes. I suppose so. Truth and healing.' As I scratched at the terrible itch.

He clicked his tongue against his teeth as he hunched over the massive steering wheel.

'Nah mate. You is just lookin' for healing I says. Truth, you don' give a rat's arse. Just the healing is.'

'No, no.' I protested. 'Healing comes from truth. Surely even you know that.'

'How the hells I know anythin' mate? I'm just drivin' and drivin'.'

'Yes, exactly! And that's where truth comes, Right? Driving and thinking? I mean surely you have found truth? Out here? Alone? Thinking?'

He looks into the beam of light that pushes before us and his face is serene.

Yes, a test.

He knows, but I must earn the truth from this strange thin priest.

After a while he hunches back into his seat and taps a finger on the steering wheel.

'Nah' he mutters. 'You don wanna truth'

'I do…' I whisper desperately 'I do want the truth.'

'Ah don' think you do.'

'I do think I do and I should know because… well, because I'm me. And I know what I want.'

He hunches forward again, his back like a lobster as he embraces the wheel of his massive rig.

'Hokay' he says to the windscreen. 'Here is a truth you don' want…'

Yes! I have passed the test. I knew it!

'Truth…' he sighs 'She is a road. Like this.'

He nods to the beam-slashed darkness and is silent.

I ponder.

'You mean it is endless and dark?'

'Nah,' he scoffs.

'Oh, I get it. Truth goes on… in a straight line… but… but we can't see it, yes, we can't see the truth until it is right before us!'

I was jubilant. Exultant. This sounded like real wisdom from a trucker priest. It felt right.

'Nah. Wot th' hell you gibberin' mate?'

I clenched a fist and held my tongue.

'Truth, mate, is like this road roight? 'Cos it is always gonna be beneath you until the day you die.'

A single straggly eyebrow raised itself from a watery eye as he looked into the looming dark.

'That is the stupidest thing I have ever heard in my whole life!'

'I don think you ever heard nothin' in you whole life mate.'

'And you must be stoned,' I grunt at him, 'because that makes no sense. And besides…'

Probably the dumbest thing to do to a long-distance trucker is question his use of performance enhancing chemicals. The thin face had drawn sharply shut and flushed deep red. So now I'm standing in the gritty dirt again as the darkness runs at me from all directions and the dozen glowing eyes on the back of Julian's curtainer fade in the shimmering velvet leaving nothing but darkness once again. Some bloody guru he turned out to be.

I listen. I scratch at the accursed rash that hovers about my hair line, the angry red burnish, a novice's skull cap, marking me clearly as unworthy. 'It's all in your head' they said. 'Just leave it, it'll go away' they insisted.

It didn't go away. It hasn't got better. It's worse. And now it burns. The cold dry air is rasping across my head. A steel-wool skull cap. I ache to scratch more but I know this will offer only a moments peace before the torment returns with even greater passion. This is the one truth I am sure of. Suddenly it seems quite logical to me that people should scratch their heads when they are puzzled. Seeking knowledge and Truth seems to be inextricably linked to the scalp. Perhaps I will have better luck if I can find a trucker priest with a suitably denuded cranium. I kick the dark sand, hear a rock skitter in the blindness. I begin walking along the hard road in the silent night, alone with my burning scalp.

The lights look… wrong. The distant whine of the exhaust and shattering air reach me long before I can see the lights. The headlights are dull, dimmed, like eyes nearing sleep, not the high beam blast of illumination needed to roar through this dark wilderness. And the truck is black. Not a sleek, sinister, glossy black. This is dull. Weathered. A battered black. A burned wreck. The whole rig reeks of ill maintenance. And hot oil. Inside it smells of curry. My feet crush a collection of aluminium foil and paper that wells in the darkness around my feet. As the truck grinds into gear and lurches back on to the highway I feel I'm traveling from bad to worse. The driver is a bulk of man, a massive belly supports the steering wheel, and his massive breasts threaten to plump from the arm holes of his sweated blue vest. A smell of vinegar and cheese waft up every time he changes gear with a wobbling arm of flab. His totally bald scalp tops a face that is surprisingly babyish. Round and quiet, relaxed, as if unaware of the mountain of sweat and fat that it is attached too.

He finally scrapes into top gear and allows his bulk to settle back, his face set in a patient, attentive gaze, his body set like jelly. The dulled headlights provide nowhere near enough illumination. I find myself constantly trying to peer into the dark, looking for the ever present 'roos that can bound frighteningly onto the highway with no warning, like a child chasing a wayward ball. The truckers, I have noticed, didn't care about the 'roos. 40 tonnes of truck doesn't even feel a hundred kilo of 'roo as it breaks it into its component molecules at over a hundred kilometres an hour. 'Roos make me jumpy though. Maybe that's Rocky's fault.

After a half hour of intent peering, I have strained my eyes to the point that they relax in spite of my attempts to see in the dark. I no longer notice the smell of curry but one of the aluminium containers seems to have become stuck to my sandshoe.

'so…' I say quietly, just above the road hum, 'You got a name?'

Humming road and baby-faced silence. And then;

'Yeah, I do Thanks.'

Outside the night remains solid and still as the truck tears headlong into a pool of its own urine yellow light.

My scalp has begun to itch again. Hot air is roiling up my legs and filling the cab, making it festering hot and wet, like the inside of a bandage. The light lilt of classical music swells and dips, sometimes light and peaceful, now stark and imposing, then back to a riverside calm of gliding strings. I silently thank the powers of the world that these truckers have grown out of country music. Somewhere behind me I hear a whirring and clicking as the CD changes. Some woman starts crooning mournfully and the baby-faced trucker taps a finger to the mordant beat.

The rash at my head burns, nagging me. At over a hundred kilometres an hour I desperately feel that I'm getting nowhere.

'So…' I begin again, 'd'you know the holy one? He's a trucker like you.'

'Whu…' he says in a soft, oddly high voice, 'you mean he's fat?'

'er, no. I mean, what I mean is… he's… oh never mind.'

The road rumbles beneath us as nothing happens all around us in deep darkness.

'What do you need a holy man for?'

'I'm… looking for some answers… is all.'

'Sounds like you need an encyclopaedia'

'Not that sort of answer. Important answers, like to big questions…'

He shrugs. I tell him;

'…you wouldn't understand.'

The air continues to shatter about us, bludgeoned by the huge square snout of the black Mack.

'What's that on your head then?' He asks without even looking at me.

I touch the burning red welts at my forehead.

'Oh, that's nothing.'

'Geez, I'm glad I haven't got 'nothing'. You look like a matchstick. All white and then red on top.'

His baby face cracks in a grin as he stares out into the distance. Looking at his eyes like this I suspect he could be completely blind. Staring without really seeing.

I stop myself from scraping at my inflamed scalp.

'Yeah, I kind of wanted to see if the holy man could fix it.'

He nods and his chin jiggles.

'Right. So this holy man is a skin doctor too eh?'

'No. I don't think so. I've seen a dermatologist, that's what we call a skin doctor in the city. He said there's nothing he can do. Same with the GP, some allergy doctor and even a woman at the chemist. No one can heal my head.'

He chewed a baby-fat lip as he stared sightlessly into the vacant heart of the desert.

'So some truck driver is going to help when all those other folks didn't?'

Staring out at the dull road, with empty food containers stuck to my feet and a man the size of his own truck sitting next to me, I see the folly of my dream. There is no truth out here that could heal me. The trucker priest was a myth, a lie, a story these bored men told each other to while away the endless, useless miles.

'You really expected a truck driver to heal you?' He asked with a tinge of mocking.

'Yeah. I guess I did.' I feel stupid.

We stared blindly into the night.

'If he could heal though, why would he bother driving a truck huh?'

I sighed, deflating.

'I figured that you guys, with all this time to just sit and think, you might know something no-one else has thought of, something special, something so enlightening and wise it would shed some light on… on my… any way. Yeah. Dumb huh?'

He grunted. Then.

'I don't know. Looking for wisdom might be the best thing you can do. Or the worst.'

'Huh?'

The rusted chrome side mirrors juddered outside the cab as they slashed through the thick night.

'What've you got to give this holy man then?' Baby face asked.

'Give him? Nothing.'

'What, you expect this guy to heal you and give you the secrets of the universe, or whatever, all the fruits of his endless hours of thinking, he's going to just give them to you, for free?'

'I…' I hadn't even thought of that 'I guess so. Yeah.'

He grunted.

He fished around beneath his ample buttocks, shifting his massive cheeks, straining at his shorts as he fumbled about. Finally he pulled out a half roll of Lifesavers. Peppermint, the dark blue packet wrinkled. With one deft but sweaty hand he stripped back the paper and offered the exposed mint to me.

I managed not to gag.

'No… thanks.'

He shrugged and flipped a mint into his mouth, his sightless eyes never wavering from their deep stare for even a moment.

The night roared about us as he sucked, little slurps and pops occasionally counter-pointing the various moans and wails from the depressed girl on the CD.

He crunched the mint and then shifted his bulk.

'.. you see…' he said, 'people've got too much imagination not to find something if they really look for it hard enough.'

I looked at his staring baby face.

'Like evolution…' he continued 'or gods. Aliens. We are so smart we can bend any facts to any truth we want.'

As I turned to face him across the cab a foil container rattled and fell from my sneaker.

'But how do you know it's truth then?'

'Because you found it.'

I thought about that a moment as a large moth blasted itself onto the cliff face of windscreen in a green brown splatter.

'That's absolute crap' I told baby face. 'That means that everything is what we want it to be!'

'Uhu' He flicked a lever and water poured onto the windscreen, washing the moth entrails into a long misty smear.

Is it irony to be in a truck hauling building supplies, being driven by a post-structuralist?

I asked Baby face, who just continued to stare blankly through the mist of insect viscera.

Eventually he replied.

'Was that a joke?'

'Yeah, I think so.' I admitted.

'I don't know what poster-whatever is but I reckon if you stop looking so hard, you'll probably find your answer anyway.'

'Oh yeah.' I sneered. 'Good advice.'

He sucked at a tooth.

'Maybe it's looking that makes you sick?'

I looked at him a moment.

I shook my head slowly, weary. What a waste. What a useless waste. Nothing was all about me. And no answers.

I had searched.

I had found.

Nothing.

My chest ached to sigh, and a desperate tightness gripped my head. I wondered if my heart would choose to stop beating now. Perhaps my brain would just stop telling it to do its job. I wouldn't mind. I really couldn't care less.

So tired, I rested my burning head on the cool glass of the side window. The glass smelled of green moss and the blurred road vanished into the black of the outback.

My eyes shut themselves. I looked across at baby face and he was asleep too. His sightless eyes were closed, his chin resting between his big momma cleavage and through the windscreen was blue sky. I should be in terror but instead I was calm. The truck roared on. Clouds were rushing past the window, a mob of kangaroos, big, red, with large happy eyes, bounded alongside and stared back at me. Beneath us was more blue sky. If the road was beneath me, I thought absently, it was a long way down. A huge white galleon of cloud loomed before us and in his sleep baby face steered the truck to avoid ploughing through its pristine whiteness. And I flew. Light, strong but weightless, I flew.

Then suddenly we were stopped, a screech of airbrakes and sleeping baby face was hauling the gear stick back as steam flowered about us, water crashed through where the windscreen should be and covered me. Warm water. He wrenched the hand brake and we stopped with a bump. My head slammed against the side window and I found darkness about me and cold saliva on my cheeks. More than dribble and cool, I realised I felt rested. An ease had loosened my skin, like a weight, lifted.

A door slammed shut and through the windshield I saw baby face's bald head bobbing off through the copper vapour lights of a truck stop. The truck idled quietly, gurgling like a little stream. Grit and dried sweat coated my skin. I had wet my pants, but I felt strangely cozy and safe inside. The granite reef of solid fear in my chest had become a marshmallow. I ran a hand through my stringed hair and found with a shock that my scalp was free of pain. No burning, no lumpy welts. I gave a little scratch and a sleepy grin tugged at my cheeks.

Amen.

An Inconsistent Line

Jeanette Barry

'So, what happened Saturday night?'

'Not much, after the movie, she hit the brakes.'

'Sucks man, or in your case I guess she didn't.' He laughed, slapping his friend on the back in mock consolation. 'Did you at least get some over-the-clothes action?'

'Enough to get me going. It was such a tease.'

Alex couldn't help but overhear their conversation in the small change rooms over the sound of the showers. He always assumed by the boisterous nature of these conversations that this was deliberate, as much about performance as the conversation between friends. It often made him wonder about the accuracy of these boasts but realistically it didn't matter to him whether it was true, the whole thing just made him uncomfortable. A constant reminder that no matter how much he tried he would never really connect with the other members of the team.

He knew they tolerated his presence out of a desire to win, after all he was the only one that could get the ball to move off a good line at pace. Ability made up for something but not for everything, he would always be on the social fringe. Left out and almost forgotten, except for game day. Realistically that was probably better than the alternatives. Pretending was hard enough already and the prospect of being invited to one of their parties created a sense of dread.

Of course, before he joined the team Alex had been all too visible for the wrong reasons, so he knew the other option only too well. Afterall, his closest friends were mostly girls, a collection of misfits interested in anime, computer games and the wildness of the romantic poets. If that hadn't been enough of a target, he foolishly decided to grow his hair out, which combined with his skinny figure meant he became a lightning rod for those looking for an easy kill. Even after cutting his hair, the names had stuck. It had been his own fault he realised, crossing the important line of expected male behaviour and the bullying was society's punishment. He was smart enough to know better and yet he asked for it.

Thankfully, Coach Ryan provided an answer through his insistence that Alex joined the team. The opportunity to exploit his love of cricket and skill with the ball to reduce the unwanted attention appealed to him. After all, once they realised he could turn a game their way with a couple of overs, self interest became a powerful motivator to encourage them to leave him alone. It had worked to a point as in public it was team first, but the change rooms were different, the best he could expect was overhearing conversations like today. Often, he had to deal with uneasy suspicion as they shot concerned looks in his direction as if he might take advantage of them. Sometimes that created a degree of outright hostility covered up with the usual false bravado of people that worried about their own sexuality. It meant that Alex occupied a weird space in the change rooms both as prey for his other teammates to ridicule and abuse but also as a threat.

Grabbing his kit, Alex was happy to be leaving the rest of the team behind, if he hurried, he would be able to catch the early train. It meant a quick sprint but that would be infinitely better than having to share a carriage with his teammates. Especially since it seemed that at least one of them might be looking for some distraction from their own frustration. Still, his aching muscles as he arrived on the platform seemed to disagree.

Once the train pulled in, he quickly slid onto a spare seat and pulled out his phone. He scanned his notifications but there wasn't much of interest. Putting in his ear pods, he sunk down into the seat and hit play. It didn't take long for the music to start easing his tension. He almost lived for these moments. The ability to block the world out but also avoid the noise of his own thoughts. It was an escape no matter how brief.

His reprieve was interrupted by a message from Vicky. *'Hey, Jock, u home soon? Need u 4 raid.'* It wasn't completely unwelcome, but he hated when she called him that, but decided to let it pass.

'On the train, give me 30.'

'When u give this shit up? Cuts into serious game time?'

'Seasons over in 4 wks.'

'So 4 wks to u stop faking it.'

'What?' He didn't really need to ask but always like to force people to actually commit to their beliefs. Even when they were going to insult him, if his temper was up, he got them to go to the extreme. They couldn't back away from it then.

'U know, getting on with those jerks.'

'and U know thats not it.'

'No more love the game BS, please. U should just watch it IMAO'

'Not the same. Besides Dad likes it.'

'U dont owe him a thing.' He knew she was right about that much but still it was nice to have something to talk about. Every week around game day they discuss tactics, balling plans, and possible field placements. It was not the mundane conversation that they normally shared around the dinner table when they both seemed to be playing a role, he could see his father's eyes light up. It was the same for him, those moments he let go everything else and he could just be genuine at least in the context of cricket. Besides it felt like proof they were related, that they could share something and he was reluctant to give that up.

'Come on, ur giving it to me about falling for expectations'

'Dont know what u mean?'

'yeah, u like hours of study'

'Work ethic is not a bad thing'

'Now, whose spinnin shit'

'Ok, u win' It was gratifying that she conceded the point, like he could tell himself that everyone lived a lie for others, even though they both knew it wasn't the same. *'All Im sayin is maybe its time to stop pretending. U deserve to be u at some point.'*

'Thats what Im doing, at least as much as I can.'

'No matter how much it puts u in the way of those thugs.'

'U saw them last year, Im already their target.'

'I know, thats why we all worry.' He didn't reply, none of this was terribly new but it was the first time that Vicky or any of his friends had really voiced it directly. They were looking out for him, but he knew they could never really understand why he would put himself in that environment. They knew the truth and helped create a space where he was safe, however they still struggled with things that didn't fit the stereotype, after all it was their only point of reference. It meant they couldn't reconcile the desire to play cricket with everything else, in some ways he struggled with it as well. At times he had trouble separating what was him and the identity he had to perform. He had spent hours dwelling on it and was no closer to really knowing himself. It struck to the very core of his being and inevitably left him feeling wretched.

He quickly sent some barely adequate acknowledgement and brought the conversation to a close. It had taken him to a place he would have rather avoided, and he needed a distraction before he got home. Scrolling through the track list he found something to take his mind of things and sank back down into the seat. It wasn't much of a solution, but it was the best he could manage. He had almost relaxed by the time the train arrived at his station, and he could see his father's car. The realisation made him tense a little.

It wasn't that long a walk home, but his father seemed to enjoy picking him up after training. Alex hoped it was to share those moments he had mentioned to Vicky but when he was being less kind, he felt that it was a form of public performance as if he was showing the world his son was normal. Struggling a little under the weight of the kit bag as he stepped off the train, he realised it didn't matter all that much, he just needed to get home, he needed the escape.

'How are you guys shaping up for the semi on the weekend?' His father asked as he threw the kit bag in the back.

'We'll be alright, James couldn't get anything out of the middle of the bat so hopefully that changes, otherwise I might actually need to bat.'

'You're good for a couple of runs,' his father chuckled, starting the car.

'Only off a thick outside edge with plenty of pace on the ball so it carries over slips.'

'You could try a novel approach and keep it along the ground.'

'We both know that's not going to happen, I'm lucky if the ball doesn't take out middle stump.'

'Well, you break through early and it won't matter.'

'There's more chance of that happening, especially if we get some cloud cover.'

'What's the plan for that opener, what's his name…'

'Davies'

'Yeah, he's pretty solid. He's the one you need to get. Even when he isn't scoring, he tends to just occupy the crease and they build the innings around him.'

'I'm going to try and really frustrate him by getting a lot to move away. Hopefully he will eventually fish at one to try and get bat-on-ball.'

'Sound plan, need to stay patient. It is going to depend on whether Rob can hold his line and back you up from the other end.'

'Steven is going to open instead and if we get the breakthrough Rob can come in and capitalise with his pace.'

'That will be a better mix, Steven will keep it tight and build the pressure. That first spell is going to be real grind with you two.' His father concluded as he pulled into the drive. The conversation ending as they left the car behind. His father completely engaged in something to do with Alex, eager to spend this time with him. It felt right in some ways. Yet wrong in others.

He wondered what went through his father's mind during these moments. Did he feel like it was a sign perhaps of some sort of change, that Alex was starting to become the son he imagined, or did he think like his friends that it was all fake. Alex hoped that deep down his father knew the truth and would be in some way prepared whenever it all came out, when Alex couldn't take it anymore. He cursed himself for the delusion. The wishful thinking was painful, it built up expectations that he knew would not be fulfilled. It was just another form of torture that Alex seemed to inflict on himself, and he had set his mind down that path.

Thankfully he was home, and he could escape online, otherwise those thoughts would fester. He didn't waste time changing, a quick wave to his mother as he ran upstairs while she still sat at her computer working and it was straight to his room. Quickly putting on his headset as the screen came to life.

A couple of clicks later and his character was dropping into the dense jungle of an alternate world where everything seemed possible. There she was, the closest thing Alex had to a representation of self and one only a few people knew about.

'*Alright Sporty Spice, we were getting sick of waiting for you.*'

A Divine Appointment

Joanna Eliott

Makarrata is a Yolgnu word for coming together after a struggle. Laura Tregonning knew nothing of the town's history and cared even less for onomastics when she boarded the ladies only train carriage at Spencer Street Station. Her only concern was to arrive at her great aunt's house with as little fanfare as possible.

Laura scanned the width of the carriage, averting her eyes from curious onlookers before finally deciding on an empty seat. Her thoughts surprisingly turned to her childhood and the many happy occasions she had spent playing 'Musical Chairs' with her classmates. Laura's physicality and athleticism had always given her a clear advantage over the other girls. As an adult, though, her physical attributes had landed her in a whole world of trouble. The music had stopped playing for Laura in 1952, and without forewarning, she found herself completely displaced.

An elderly woman cocked her head as Laura gravitated to the seat beside her. 'Good morning, dear.'

'Good morning,' Laura replied politely as she peered out from under her mushroom-styled summer hat. The elderly woman was dressed in traditional clothing which conformed to the social norms of the day, without attracting any unnecessary attention. She was part of a generation that existed to serve, not to be served.

'Where are you travelling to, today, my dear?' she asked in a warm and gentle voice.

'Makarrata.'

'Oh my! That's where I'm going! I live there, you see, with Norman and our cat, Tabby.'

'That's nice.' Laura returned the smile.

'Is it your first time, visiting Makarrata? Where are you staying?'

'Yes, it's my first visit. I'm staying with my Mum's great aunt Clara. You see… Mum arranged everything,' Laura's voice trailed off.

'Ahhh. I know Clara very well. Why, she's just a stone's throw away from us! I'm Elva, by the way. What's your name, dear?'

'It's Laura. Laura Tregonning.'

'So lovely to meet you, Laura Tregonning. And I get to have your company for the next three hours. How fortunate for me! I'm sure that we're going to get along like a house on fire.' Elva squeezed Laura's gloved hands as they rested on her lap.

'TICKETS PLEASE.'

Conductor Mark Price could almost be mistaken for Mr. Moon opening his giant mouth to Luna Park, beckoning his patrons on to what would surely be a thrilling ride. Laura was grateful for the sight of him and turned her attention to her purse, carefully extracting her flimsy ticket. The conductor grinned sheepishly at her, barely able to conceal his delight at discovering this delectable creature before him. The young lady was certainly a change from the venerable types he usually met on the Melbourne to Mansfield route, a rural outpost which was as uninteresting a place as could be. In his considerable experience, the area singularly attracted mature-aged women who had been visiting their five generations of family and could think of nothing better than returning to their ancestral homes for some well-earned rest and recuperation.

'Thank you, Miss!'

As he punched Laura's ticket in a theatrical manner, Conductor Mark tried his hardest to appear composed and natural. He racked his brain to think of something interesting to say to her, and was just able to open his mouth to speak when the elderly woman sitting nearby began to mutter to herself. She then started to empty all the contents of her handbag onto her lap and wave her bag about, checking every inch and fold of the black lizard skin-looking contraption. Conductor Mark reluctantly turned to the vexed passenger:

'Is there a problem, Madam?'

'Why yes, you see, I cannot find my ticket. I know I purchased it last week and put it right here in my bag's front pocket, but look…there's nothing there!' With this she thrust open the handbag so that the Conductor could examine it for himself. The satin lining pocket was indeed empty.

'Are you sure you purchased a ticket, Madam?'

'Young man, I can assure you that I did! I was visiting my cousin Mabel in Albert Park, as I do every year on her birthday, and I always keep my important documents right here.' She patted the bag's compartment before carefully checking each item again, just like a shopkeeper who knew their products back to front. 'This has never happened to me before…' She felt a deep sense of shame.

'I'm sorry, Madam, but if you can't produce a numbered ticket, I am going to have to ask you to vacate this seat.'

The train was moving at a steady pace and the densely populated city streets gradually morphed into sparse green fields. As interesting as the scenery was, it proved to be no match for the onboard entertainment. Everyone's eyes were firmly fixed on the elderly lady and the drama unfolding before them.

'Madam, I must ask you to come with me now, and find a seat elsewhere.'

'I'm very sorry. I…. don't know how this could have happened.' Elva hurriedly placed her knitting needles, ball of red wool, brown leather coin purse and a giant magnifying glass back into her bag, before gripping the metal railing in front of her and slowly lifting herself up. Her whitened knuckles mirrored her now ghost-white countenance.

'Please, there's no need for that! She can have my seat. I don't mind travelling in third class.'

Laura was embarrassed by the sound of her own voice. She didn't relish the thought of standing up again, nor travelling in a third-class carriage for that matter. The type of passenger inhabiting third-class accommodations did not bear thinking about, especially in her current condition. She could almost hear the strong disapprobation of her mother, a woman who had devoted her life to making Laura into a proper little lady, including sending her to June Daly Watkins' Finishing School in Sydney.

'Ah. Um. Miss, this is highly irregular,' stammered the Conductor, scratching his head. He hated to be at odds with such an agreeable sort.

Elva turned to Laura and smiled weakly. 'My dear. I would not hear of it. I do thank you for your kindness though. It is most appreciated, but I must take my lumps, you see....' She touched Laura's arm lightly before heading out the door, under the helpful escort of the officious Conductor. The carriage breathed a collective sigh of relief as the train hurtled onwards, almost like it, too, was trying to forget its past sins.

As she stared out the window, Laura noticed the barren plains of North Eastern Victoria interspersed by tall red gums dotted along the surrounding grey hills. The sky was blue and cloudless, Laura's favourite type of sky. She noticed a black and white border collie circling a flock of merino sheep. She thought the dog was just like a VFL field umpire running around the team, enjoying the best view of the play as he herded both the stragglers and the leaders.

Lost in her own thoughts, it wasn't long before Laura heard the whistle blow for Makarrata Station. All the ladies remained seated while Laura collected her personal possessions and exited the carriage. Once clear of the train, she looked around for Elva but couldn't see her anywhere, so continued along the length of the platform.

'Laura Tregonning?' a man's voice enquired.

Laura turned around to face the stranger. 'Yes, that's me.'

'G'day, Miss. The name's Tom.' He squinted as he looked up from under his Akubra and offered Laura his hand in greeting. 'Your great aunt asked me to collect you from the station and drive you to the homestead.'

Tom's neat grey hair matched his blue flannel shirt tucked inside his working jeans. He looked older than what he probably was, his lined skin being the first casualty of the great Australian sun. Laura had been told to expect 'Tom' and was relieved to see him. She smiled warmly and handed him her carry bag as they walked towards one of the few vehicles parked adjacent to the station, a Ford ute complete with a cattle dog in the back tray.

'Norman! I have some exciting news! Where are you?'

As Elva entered the rear of the shop, she discovered Norman polishing up some of his latest acquisitions.

'Mum? Why didn't you tell me that you were coming home today? I would've met you at the station!'

'Never mind that now. It's not a long walk in this glorious sunshine. Besides, I needed to stretch my legs at any length.' The walk had also helped Elva recover from the indignity of the lost ticket, but she didn't feel the need to burden Norman with all that 'silliness'. 'Anyways... I met a lovely girl on the train. She's the one for you, Norman! Her name is Laura, and she's the most beautiful girl I've ever met, both inside and out!'

'Oh Mum. Why would this girl want to marry me?'

Norman had lived long enough to recognise his marriage prospects were next to nil. His social circle, what remained of the few classmates who hadn't ventured into the big smoke, or been killed in the last war, characterised him as 'Norman the nutter', not because of any neuroticism on his part. Conversely, he was probably the most emotionally stable of the lot, having been rejected for active service in WW2 on three separate occasions. His first rejection related to his poor teeth. On his second attempt, Norman learnt that he was underdeveloped. On his third and final attempt, the recruiters informed Norman that he had substandard physique. It proved to be of no great surprise to Norman (or anyone else, for that matter). Consequently, he had stayed at home with his mum, running the family business, a second-hand 'bits and bobs' store. The shop was more of a salvage shed than anything else. Norman, however, was extremely proud of his collection, and believed that he now possessed the largest selection of chicken wire in the entire state of Victoria.

'Laura is staying up at Samaritis, with Clara. Why don't we pay them a call later today, if you're up to it? Listen here, we could freshen ourselves up… and I'll cut some flowers from the garden to take with us! The marigolds and pansies are looking especially lovely, despite the heat.'

Norman knew that once his mother had set her mind upon a certain course of action, it was pointless to try to dissuade her. On many occasions, Norman had been 'invited' to participate in these casual meetings. Unsurprisingly, they all followed a similar pattern. His stomach would play up something awful, his mum would then monopolise the conversation with the intended party (and refer to Norman in the most glowing terms, of course) while the girl would smile politely and look askance. Privately, Norman had resigned himself to bachelorhood. He was completely comfortable with the concept. Actually, it afforded Norman the time to devote to important things, like collecting objects which others rejected, and brandishing them into useful and valuable things that everyone could admire. That was his calling, he felt.

Four generations had occupied and farmed the land at Samaritis. Clara, being a spinster and the sole surviving member of her generation, had managed the sheep and wool business quite ably with the help of Tom and other loyal members of her household staff. God-fearing and community-minded, Clara had been quick to answer the distressed call from her favourite niece. Clara was informed that Laura, now twenty-one and unmarried, was with child and sought refuge away from the attachments of the city and the judgemental attitudes pervading their extensive social circle. Both practically minded women imagined that Laura could make a fresh start for herself in the country, and perhaps in time, engage in some honourable work as she had studied both elocution and typing. We will soon sort this matter out. Clara glanced at the wall clock apprehensively.

When she heard the ute bearing down the pebbled driveway, she went to meet Laura at the back door. She hoped Laura would feel entirely at home in this stately residence constructed with red bricks sourced from local quarries, with its four chimneys each chewing through copious amounts of iron bark and red gum, felled from along the creek.

'Welcome, my dear! You must be tired after your long journey.' Aunt Clara pecked her grandniece on the cheek and beckoned her inside.

'Yes, it was pretty tiring, but I'm here now.' Laura tried to keep her tone positive and light hearted, a key lesson that had been drilled into her at the finishing school.

'Would you like to take a bath, dear? Then perhaps we can have a cup of tea and get reacquainted before dinner?'

'That sounds lovely. Thanks, Aunt Clara.'

Once Clara had shown Laura up to her bedroom, a cheerful room of generous proportions and botanically-inspired wall paper, she left her to settle in. Laura immediately looked out the window and noticed the colonial-style veranda encircling the upper decking. As she stepped onto the veranda all her senses were engulfed by the perfume emanating from the garden and the lyrical birdsong. Laura so wished to be a part of it! Without a moment's hesitation, she headed back downstairs, into the elegant foyer, and out through the heavy front door. Once outside, she followed the trail towards the creek which eventually took her to the forest road. On one side of the road, gargantuan cows sauntered towards the barbed wire fence as they tried to get a proper look at their visitor. Reticent sheep had taken up residence across the road from the cows. Keeping one eye on Laura, and another on their lush green pastureland, they continued to graze away unperturbed by her presence. Suddenly, Laura spotted a little white chapel on the hilltop. She wondered what it was like inside, and made a mental note to head straight back to Samaritis… just as soon as she had visited the quaint little chapel.

'What's that sound Norman?'

'Not sure, Mum. I think the engine might have overheated. I'll need to stop and take a proper look.'

'Oh dear! Why did this have to happen now of all times? We're so close. I can practically see Samaritis from here!'

'Well, it can't be helped, I'm afraid,' Norman said as he pulled over. 'Hey, I've got an idea! Why don't you go without me?' Norman stole a quick glance at his mother.

'What do you mean, Norman?'

'Well, I could be here fixing the car for hours. There's no point in you wasting your time, waiting with me. Why don't you visit with Clara… on your own?' Norman half expected a clip behind the ears.

'Actually, that's not altogether a bad notion! I could prepare the groundwork, so to speak. You could then swing past, whenever you finish, and collect me. Then I could explain what a clever boy you are, fixing all manner of things.'

'Yep. Sounds like a plan alright, Mum.'

Norman couldn't help thinking that God had somehow intervened to spare him yet another round of humiliating encounters. Who says that the Lord doesn't answer the prayers of the faithful? He mused.

Once his mother had ambled off, flowers in hand, Norman popped open the car bonnet to check the oil and water levels. To his chagrin, he discovered a leak in the system. He moistened his lips with his tongue, knowing that the car desperately needed water, and wondered where the closest water source could be… other than Samaritis, of course. Suddenly, he remembered the little white chapel. It had a front garden. It must have a water tap! With renewed vigour, Norman headed towards the chapel to search for the tap.

A short time later, as he was scurrying around the shrubs and overgrown bushes, Norman was startled by the sound of a woman's voice:

'Hi there. Are you looking for something?' Laura's lips twisted into a wry smile as she watched Norman crawling around on all fours.

'Oh, I didn't see you there. My car has broken down nearby. I need to get some water into her, to help cool her down.'

'I see. Can I help in any way?'

'Um, maybe. I'll need something to carry the water back to the car.'

Laura thought for a moment, and quickly returned with a flower vase she had spotted inside the vestry.

'That's perfect. Thanks so much,' Norman exclaimed, accepting the vase from her.

'No problem', she replied.

Norman quickly filled the vessel with water, and headed off.

'Hey, I'll walk with you, if you don't mind. I'm going in the same direction,' Laura called out after him.

'Oh, right.'

Norman treaded cautiously so as not to spill any of the precious cargo. Laura enjoyed the unhurried pace. After a few moments, Norman broke the ice by saying:

'Hey, you remind me of the Samaritan woman at the well, you know, when Jesus asked a stranger for a cup of water, and ended up offering her life-giving water?'

Laura knew the story quite well and began to blush. The reference was a little too close to the bone.

When he heard no response, Norman glanced across at Laura and saw her face reddening.

'Hey, I'm sorry. I didn't mean anything by that. I was just referring to the fact that you were standing near the tap when I needed some water... Please forgive me if I misspoke. You're nothing like the Samaritan woman, really!'

'Actually,' Laura stammered, 'I have a great deal in common with her.'

Norman stopped and turned to face her. Laura looked down at her feet and shifted uncomfortably for a moment. When she finally met his gaze, she noticed that his eyes were filled with compassion. As she allowed herself time to examine his face more closely, Laura was struck by something else. This man possessed the rarest of qualities: kindness in its purest sense. Overcome with emotion, she began to sob.

Norman was taken aback by her reaction but instinctively placed his arms around her and held her. And while the feel of a lady's embrace was completely foreign to him, Norman felt strangely calm. Norman's chest size was perfectly suited to hold Laura.

When Laura's tears finally subsided, Norman peered into her face but didn't speak. He figured she would talk when she was ready.

'Would you like to sit down in the field?' he enquired softly.

Laura just nodded. She followed Norman over to a shady patch of grass and sat down beside him. The vase of water had long been forgotten.

In due course, Laura began to share her story:

'I haven't told anyone, yet. My mum knows some of it, but not all of it. Last year, I was working as a secretary for the head of corporate affairs of National Insurance Limited. Things were ok at the start, but then my boss started to expect me to work longer and longer hours. He could be quite nice at times, and suddenly turn into an angry bear without any provocation. Anyway, whenever I questioned him about anything, he would remind me of how lucky I was that I had the senior secretary's position, without any real experience.' Laura creased her brow before continuing. 'One evening, we were working late, and he offered me a drink. As he was already drinking, I thought it impolite to decline, so I took some spirits. Next thing I knew, he was all over me. As much as I tried, I couldn't push him away.' Her eyes filled with tears again.

Norman didn't know where to look. He was both saddened and angered by the revelation, in equal measure. When she had finished speaking, he uttered:

'I am so sorry this happened to you.'

Laura took his hand and squeezed it. 'You know, I can't believe I just told a complete stranger my whole life story! All of the bad bits, at least,' she chuckled. 'Thank you for hearing me out.'

'Not sure if I did that much,' Norman grinned.

They sat companionably for a while, looking across at the panoramic vistas and enjoying the sound of a bird chanting some little song.

Norman finally broke the silence. 'You know, all of us have battles to face...' Laura studied him closely, marvelling at the hidden depths of this man. '…but I think we find strength in honesty.' He winked at her.

'Well, I have no choice, really. I can't pretend this didn't happen. A new life is on its way!' Laura exhaled deeply and patted her stomach.

'Well, it sounds to me that something good, may come out of something very bad,' Norman smiled reassuringly.

Laura liked the sound of that. It was a very positive outlook. The teachers at June Daly Watkins' Finishing School would be suitably impressed! A smile crossed her lips.

'What's so funny?' Norman asked her.

'Nothing really. It's just that I don't even know your name.'

'Fair enough. Ok, why don't we do this properly? Norman held out his hand. 'Hello there. My name's Norman. Nice to finally meet you!'

'Hello, Norman. It's nice to meet you too. By the way, I'm Laura.'

Norman stared at her incredulously. Laura smiled coyly, recognising that in that moment, she felt a sense of happiness and peace like never before.

The Afterlife

Erin A. Mitchell

Part One

The End

A jogger found me in the bush. Well, he found my body. If he'd seen me, I think he might have had a heart attack. Or be involuntarily hospitalised in a mental health facility. Finding what was left of me after the attack, and the animal predation in the days since, was traumatising enough. I can't imagine what seeing my ghost, or spirit, or whatever I am now, would have done to him.

The jogger has a dog with him. Technically it was the pooch that found me. Its sense of smell being far more sensitive and advanced than a human's. It pulled the owner towards me and, finally, after days of being alone in this bush, I was discovered. The dog came straight up to me, the real me, not the body, and whined gently. I think it was trying to say it was sorry. When the jogger realised what he was looking at, he screamed and threw up. I don't blame him. It's not a pretty sight.

Though the retching has ceased, he's still freaking out. He keeps saying "oh help me god" over and over. Like some deity is going to respond to the person who finds the murdered victim and not, you know, the actual victim. I want to feel something for him. Sympathy. Empathy. Anything. But all I can muster up is cool detachment. It seems weird that his reaction to finding my dead body is more extreme than my own reaction to dying.

I don't remember what came before. Or how I came to be in the reserve a few blocks away from my home. My body is clad in ripped jogging gear and dirty running shoes. I'm not a runner, or a jogger. But I like to walk through the parklands. I like visiting the curious but cautious Eastern Grey kangaroos that live nearby. Taking binoculars so I can bird watch, or spot rabbits in the brush. Sorry, liked. It'll take some getting used to the whole past tense when it comes to my life. Even more so since I'm inexplicably still here. I remember my life. My family. Friends. Childhood. School. University. Finding a decent job, but ultimately unsure if it's what I wanted to do forever. I guess I don't have to worry about any of that now.

The moments before my death are blank. One minute I lay there amongst the dewy autumn leaves, with the earthy smell of dirt, grass, and blood around me. And the next I was apart. Separate. Outside of my body. I don't remember being attacked. Nor who, or what, attacked me. I assume it was violent, judging by the state of my body. Perhaps it's a good thing that I have no memory of it.

There was no bright light. No sign pointing up or down. My life did not flash before my eyes. Which, may I add, is extremely disappointing and I would seek to formally complain to Hollywood, and every other film and television production company around the world for the misleading expectation, if I wasn't, you know, dead.

In the moments since becoming aware of my new reality, I thought about venturing out of the shrubbery and into the more populated areas of the parklands. Not for me, obviously, since it was far too late for that. But for my body. For my family. No doubt my parents would want to have a funeral. Closure. I'm not sure if it was fear or resignation that kept me away from the living. Ultimately, I stayed behind and waited. I didn't know what else to do.

I hadn't given much thought as to how I would die. I knew it was coming. It comes for us all. I never had a fear of death, or of losing loved ones. Maybe that made me a bit of a sociopath, but I think it's a healthy outlook on life. One that encourages you to cherish and celebrate the good stuff while you can. I never thought it would happen in my early thirties.

The jogger has composed himself now and is on the phone to 000. His dog is sitting next to me, I can't touch it of course, but it's comforting all the same. Pretty soon all this bushland will be filled with police officers, looky-loos, and possibly even the media. Disturbing all the peace and trampling the homes of the animals and plants that live here. I just want to go home. Away from this mess.

A numbness washes over me as I sit down next to my body. Though it's more of a vague approximation of sitting since I can't actually feel the ground beneath me. It's a surreal experience. As is being conscious and aware that I am here and whole, though invisible. But I'm also down there. Battered. Bruised. Covered in blood. When I reach out and touch my hand, I can feel grit beneath my fingernails. The incorporeal ones. I lean in to inspect my physical hand and see a combination of dirt, leaves, and tan bark under the nail beds. Flashes of the afterwards come at me through the contact.

Clawing at the ground. Clenching through the pain wracking my body. Clinging to my fading life.

I lift my hand and the sensation is gone. Returning to the humming numbness of before. Next, I place a hand on my leg. I can feel a cut in my calf. My pants cover where it's located, but I can feel it against the material of my incorporeal leg. It's like my spirit self can feel what the body still feels. Though it shouldn't be feeling anything anymore. Perhaps it's the connection between mind, body, and soul. Perhaps it's the last message my peripheral nervous system tried to communicate to my central nervous system before it all collapsed. Either way, it's too confronting so I fold my arms across my chest instead.

Whatever I am now, I still feel solid to myself. I just wish I knew why I was still here.

Part Two
The Investigation

The little bushland where my body lay by itself is now full of people. Uniformed police officers, detectives in suits, forensic officers in PPE. Blue and white police tape closes off the whole section of shrubbery. Someone took the jogger and his dog home a while ago and I miss the comforting whine of the canine. The Victoria Police dog squad are now on duty. I know they can sense me. However, they offer no support.

I'm surrounded by people and yet I'm all alone.

The forensic officers are working on my body. They have cameras and various tools and equipment. I watch as they gently lift my hands and scrape under my nails. I like to think their tenderness is out of respect, but I'm sure it's more about protecting the evidence. At first I moved out of the way to let them work, then I realised that I couldn't obstruct them if I tried. Now, I'm sitting where I was before. Craving the sensation of feeling something. Anything. Even pain would be better than this perpetual crushing numbness.

The officer moves over to my other hand and I reach out my corresponding incorporeal one, shaping my fingers into the same position that she's holding my real ones. A scalpel scrapes under the nails, removing the dirt and whatever else that's under there. It's as gentle as it looks. If I closed my eyes, I could almost imagine that I was getting a manicure. Almost.

They've taken their pictures and collected whatever they could from around my body and now a team of them work to turn me over. One of the uniformed officers, a younger looking man yet to outgrow the baby fat on his face, lets out a loud gasp.

'Jesus,' says another of the uniformed officers. A young-looking woman with bright red hair. 'Look at what they did to her.'

I don't look. I already know what they're seeing. I've felt them every time I've touched my body. I just didn't want to think about it. I don't remember the knife. Nor who wielded it. But every time I make contact with my body, I feel every single one of those wounds. They burned at first, like hot pokers. However, with each touch, the pain diminishes. I'm not sure if it's the nerve endings giving out, or if it's because the messages have been received. I only have a rudimentary understanding of biology and physiology and none of it covered the afterlife. And it's not like I can ask anyone here.

A crashing sound comes from beyond the tree line. Voices interrupt the calm evidence-gathering procession around me. I look away from my body and see several of the police officers making their way through the brush towards the noise. An older man puts a probe in my body's abdomen. From years of watching police procedural dramas on television, I assume he's the medical examiner. I'm so distracted by the commotion beyond the trees, that I barely feel the pinch. I only notice its absence once I pull my hand away and get up to see what's going on.

'I guess the circus is here, my dear. The vultures have come to get a glimpse of you.'

For a split second I think he's talking to me. I whip around to face him, wide-eyed and something akin to hope ballooning in my chest. It deflates when I see that he's only talking to my body. The numbness sets back in as I move away from him. Away from me.

One reporter and a cameraman are setting up in the parklands. I imagine that more will turn up as word spreads of yet another woman being attacked and killed and dumped. Or is it so commonplace now that the attention only lasts a few measly hours before the next victim is found and the cycle starts all over again. In my own life, I remember news reports on the radio on the commute to work. A one liner, usually in the B or C block. Tragedies embedded into the small margins, just above sports. The reporter is arguing with the baby-faced police officer while two detectives block the cameraman.

'Mate, please just let us get a shot of some unis, detectives, or forensics or something. They can be canvassing the area or whatever. My boss wants an exclusive.'

'You know as well as I do that I can't let you in there. Your boss is going to have to wait for the official statement like everyone else,' Baby-Face says.

'Come on mate! We can wait for you to cover the remains up.'

One of the detectives snaps his head around at the reporter, 'That's a person in there. With family and friends. People who will miss and grieve over the loss of life here. They are not remains. Show some fucking respect.'

The reporter looks down at his shoes. A light blush appears on his cheeks despite the layers of make-up that's caked on his face. 'We're the only ones here. We're the only ones who came. That has to count for something, right?'

The other detective sighs. He's older than the one who just spoke. Lines etch his face and his hair is beginning to thin. 'I get that you have a job to do, so do we. And we can't do it if we have to babysit you lot at the crime scene. Go back to your news van, and we'll check with our superiors to see what they'll allow. But I make no promises.'

If it were up to me, I'd broadcast the whole lot. Maybe if people saw the brutality of violence, more would be done to stop it.

They finally finish up and load my body into a van. I lay down on the gurney, right on top of myself, and feel the blanket covering me. The thin padding underneath. As the doors are closing, I see the reporter and the cameraman in the carpark. I guess they got their shot.

Part Three
Is this Purgatory?

Time passes differently here. It's kind of like a motion capture camera. Only activating when there's something moving around. The first few days I spent lying in the morgue drawer with my body. Feeling the cold and the dark through the still functioning senses. In the past, I'd had the odd nightmare about being stuck in one of these fridges, but the reality was more like a sensory deprivation tank. Without the floating of course.

Occasionally I popped out of my drawer to explore the facility. Being incorporeal, I can't open the drawer myself, however, I have discovered that I can move through walls and doors. It took a few tries to train my mind to do it, but I've got the hang of it now. The floors are solid. I can't exactly feel them, but I also don't float like an unhinged Hollywood ghoul. Walls provide some resistance. Pushing through them is what I imagine pushing through jelly might be like. Doors and windows however, are as insubstantial as I am.

I don't watch the autopsies. I'd always found the staged ones on tv to be gory and gross, so when my own one came around, I took that as my cue to be elsewhere for a few hours. Plus, I didn't want to risk being in proximity to my body. The compulsion for feeling, for whatever facsimile of life touching my body brings, was increasing and I did not want to feel scalpels or organ removal. Even imagining it made my head spin. If I still had a working stomach, I'm sure I would have thrown up. Besides, I don't really care to find out how I died. It makes absolutely no difference to me.

There's a small room down the hallway with a couch, two armchairs, and a small wooden coffee table. It looks like it might be a place for people to use when identifying loved ones. Light filters from a solitary fluorescent fixture and a small window that looks out onto a laneway.

Pamphlets from local funeral homes and counselling services line a rack on one wall, while a clock and a small wall-mounted tv line the other. Despite the cheerfulness of the pastel mint wall and pastel yellow seating, the room screams grief. Despite the screaming grief, it seems like an ideal place to sit and wait out my autopsy. And it is, right up until the moment my parents walk in.

Judy and Manu are in their 70s. They had me late in life, after wasting years in loveless first marriages and finding each other post-divorce in their 40s. I am their first, and only, child. And now I'm gone. The older detective from my crime scene and a woman in a suit follow them in, sitting down in the armchairs. My parents, who are clasped so tightly to each other that they can't walk straight, take the couch.

Faint mascara flecks track down Mum's face. A handkerchief is twisted within her clenched fist. I can just make out Dad's initials embroidered in the corner that sticks out above her thumb.

I don't know how travel works in this afterlife that I have found myself in, but I know that if I can travel by van, I can probably travel by car too. I walk out of the meeting. I don't want to hear what the police officer and the suited lady have to say to my parents. I don't want to see my parent's reactions to the information.

I walk outside and find my way to their car, sitting in the back middle seat like I used to as a child. I wait for them to come and take me home.

Part Four
Funerals are for the Living

My parents save a space for me at every meal. They agree on everything for my service. They fall asleep holding each other, as tears snake down their faces, wetting the pillowcases beneath them. They show no indication that they know I'm here, other than Mum commenting that she "feels my presence." I think it's more wishful thinking than an actual feeling. Dad talks to me like he talks to his roses. Softly. Quietly. And in Spanish. Family, friends, and neighbours visit my folks to pay their respects. They bring flowers and food. Small comforts for such large grief.

On the day of the service, they ride alone in a rented town car behind my hearse. Well almost alone, there's a driver and I'm there with them too. They say nothing, and yet their silence speaks volumes.

More people turn up to my funeral than I think I knew while I was alive. There's family of course. And my parent's various groups. Dad's fellow church members. Mum's sewing friends. My groups are there too. Walking. Bird watching. My friends. Colleagues. Old Uni mates. Book club. They're all here. Sitting in their separate little factions. Like high school cliques.

I am the common denominator for all of these people, and yet I had never drawn them all together while living. I spent my 30th in Thailand with my best mate. I've never been married. Or engaged. My last boyfriend was over a year ago. I hate housewarmings because they usually mean one heck of a clean up the next day. Past the age of 21, I had never had a big party for any occasion. All my groups were isolated. Compartmentalised. With the barest of crossovers. I guess you don't realise how many people are in your life until you see them all congregated in one place.

Once the service starts, I lay down with my body in the casket. It's closed, but the padding underneath me is soft and the darkness of the wooden lid is comforting. I feel weightless as I'm lifted and placed back into the hearse. I try and picture who the pallbearers are. I can hear them crying and sniffling on either side of me. I don't look though. I loved a lot of these people dearly while I was alive, now that love hurts. Them, not me. I can no longer feel much of anything. The nerves are dying. The sensations are fading. The connection is dissipating.

I listen as clods of dirt are thrown onto the coffin. Once the patter stops, when the footsteps have faded, when the sniffling and whispering of my parents is gone, I rise up from the darkness and into the late afternoon sun.

Part Five
Come meet others who can't move on

The world is different from this side. I see people rushing to work, to school, to the train that's closing its doors and leaving the platform. I have nowhere to go and nothing to rush to.

The sun is shining. Bringing out that early summer heat that hints of long days and warm nights spent outdoors on decks, or in courtyards. Not that I can feel it. My tether to this world, to the physical sensations is gone now. But I can see it in the air. In the activity of the bees and the butterflies. In the people. The masses who are spilling out of Flinders Street Station. A mix of cricket fans going out and 9-5ers heading home, reminding me that the daily grind still grinds on without me.

As I make my way along Swanston Street, people see through me. Walk through me. Life as an introvert taught me how to be invisible when I wasn't feeling sociable. Life in this afterlife is one of perpetual invisibility. Nothing prepared me for this numbness. This loneliness.

I stayed with my parents for a while. Then visited other friends or family, but didn't see the point in continuing. I spent Christmas alone despite being surrounded by family. I tried shouting. I tried screaming. I tried pushing things over and slamming doors. None of it worked. And watching my parents slowly come out of their grief-filled funk and re-engage with life was too hard.

I wish I wasn't so alone. I assume that there are others like me, although for the life of me, or the death or me, really, I can't work out why they're hidden. For a brief moment I wonder if I should just head home. Even if my folks can't see me, being around them might make things a little less lonely. I begin to turn in the direction of the station, craving the comfort only loving parents can give you. Then I see him.

He has sandy blonde hair and looks to be in his late 20s. Where the people around him are bright and vibrant, full of life, he's faded. Like an old photograph. Instantly, I know he's like me. A left over. A remnant. Trapped here for whatever reason. He smiles when he notices me looking at him and makes his way over.

'Hey, I'm Caleb,' he says, holding out his hand.

I stare at it. The habit formed during life would be to reach out and shake it. Only now, after a while of being incorporeal I've learned that I can't touch anyone.

Caleb smiles and lets out a chuckle. 'You're still new to this I see. We're corporeal to each other.'

I look at his face. It's earnest, with just a hint of mirth at the corners of his eyes and mouth.

Tentatively, I reach out my hand and feel solid human flesh and bones. In a fit of delight, I shout and throw my arms around his solid human body.

Caleb laughs and awkwardly returns my hug.

'What are we? Where are we? Why are we here? How has this happened?' I ask in a rush once I pull away. 'Sorry, you're the first person I've spoken to in months.'

'It's okay. We've all been there. What's your name?'

'Prue.'

'It's nice to meet you, Prue. We call ourselves souls. Some of us move on, some of us get stuck here in this afterlife. We don't know why it happens, only that we're still here.'

'So, there's others like us?'

'Of course there are. In fact, I'm headed to meet a few of them now. You're welcome to come and join us if you want. All your questions, and more, will be answered.'

'Why couldn't I see anyone before?'

'It takes time. We need to adjust to this life before we can be open to interactions with others. Death is a lot to process, especially if you're somewhat still alive.'

'Okay,' I say to him.

'Okay?' He asks. 'Okay. Let's go.'

Caleb smiles and leads me towards La Trobe Street. We swing into Melbourne Central a few minutes later. I've always loved the history of this building. The bricked Shot Tower encased inside the conical glass roof. The levels of floors, above and below. There are people everywhere. Coming in and out of the shops, the movies, the railway system deep underground. Caleb leads us down the escalators and just when I think we're about to go through the turnstiles and into the train station, he hangs a left and the sight of a multitude of cuisines appears before us. Layers of conversations are happening all over the place with the sounds of a piano being expertly played to everyone. And to no one.

A group of people, souls, are sitting at two adjacent booth seats. They're in and among the living, breathing, folk. Who, of course, have no idea that they, we, are even here.

'You guys meet in the food court at Melbourne Central?' I ask Caleb.

Caleb laughs. He has such an easy nature about him. So full of life. It's hard to wrap my head around the fact that he isn't actually alive. None of these people are, including myself. And yet, they're all joking and laughing like living in this afterlife doesn't bother them. Like it's normal. And I guess it is for them. Perhaps with time, that will be me too, welcoming some other new soul who stayed instead of moving on.

'Sometimes,' Caleb says, bringing my attention away from the group and back to him. 'Sometimes we meet at the footy, or the convention centre, or even the Show. Anywhere that has large numbers of people. It helps us to feel like we're all still a part of something.'

We walk over to the group and Caleb says, 'Hey everyone, this is Prue. Prue, meet the ones who stayed behind.'

The group beams up at me with warm, open faces. Some get out of their seats to hug me.

Some greet me with handshakes or enthusiastic waves. All of them smile.

The thing about finding your people is that you feel a sense of belonging. A sense of community.

A few of the group members shuffle aside to make room for Caleb and I. As he goes around the group introducing me to everyone, I realise that I am no longer alone.

I am home.

The Worst Job In the World

Charles Corkery

'Hello. Welcome. Please remove any jewellery or metal objects. Please remove all clothing and, when you're ready, step back outside. Thank you.'

The long dark haired, pretty faced medical orderly smiled reassuringly at the latest patient as she took the name tag the old woman handed her and ticked off the name on her clipboard.

The gold coloured, metal badge pinned to the medical assistant's white coat read Reza. Reza's voice generator, programmed to mimic human speech, warbled slightly, the only sign that she was, in fact, an android.

As the old woman exited the cubicle, dressed only in a disposable, paper gown, she was greeted by a tall, blonde, handsome, male assistant, also dressed in a white lab coat, whose own gold coloured, metal name badge said Ezra.

'Hello. How are you, today? Now, can I just get you to lie down on the bed with your feet on the red line. Excellent. Well done. Now, relax your head. Perfect. Now, I'm going to pull down the canopy. Can you still hear me? Good. You'll hear some music in a moment. Just relax and enjoy.'

Ezra stepped away from the pod and pressed a button on the side of the computerised machine. The old woman, eviscerated, simply disappeared. Ezra waited just a moment, then lifted the canopy releasing a slight stench of burning flesh. He pressed another button activating a powerful, hydraulic exhaust fan that swiftly sucked up the odour before reverse releasing a fragrant puff of sweet smelling pot pourri. Ezra took a hygienic wipe from a box and wiped down the bed, switched off the exhaust and signalled vocally to Reza that he was ready.

'Next.'

This time, it was a man who entered the operating theatre. He was strongly built, full head of hair and looked nowhere near the age of seventy. He handed his name tag to Reza.

'Hello. Welcome. Please remove any jewellery or metal objects…'

That night, after the Tasty Clinic had closed, the two droids sat together in silence in the charging room, the seperate leads from a generator plugged into each of their torsos With their clothing removed, their polyurethane carcasses were fully exposed; with each part of their meticulously crafted frames perfectly replicating human form. At the end of each working day, they would sit like this all night and, on a signal from the generator that they had been fully re-charged, would rise and prepare for yet another day's 'work.'

'Work' entailed the disposal of human beings who had reached the age of seventy and the line of mandatory euthanasia patients each day was carefully calculated to achieve the required daily quota decreed by the state. Hundreds of these clinics, long in the planning, had sprung up overnight across the country following the passing of the new law; a move felt necessary in order to control the ever increasing population growth of the planet. Due to the reference to the biblical life term allotted to man: Three Score Years And Ten, the public had quickly taken these letters and ascribed the anagram of TASTY to such places of mortality; a quirky indicator, both, of humans' morbid sense of humour and their ability, after the initial protests, to lapse into acceptance of their inevitable fate.

Special machines, designed and built to implement these disposals, as swiftly and painlessly as possible, had been secretly lying in warehouses for months awaiting the green light.

Everything, it seemed, had been carefully pre-planned by the powers that be but, unfortunately, nobody had calculated the reaction of human healthcare assistants to their grisly task and the psychological trauma, leading to mass absenteeism, was something totally unexpected. AI companies, ever alert, had seized the opportunity to replace those real life clinical assistants with robots able to perform their roles unemotionally and even far more efficiently.

Ezra was startled to hear Reza stir beside him. This was most unusual. Turning his head, he saw her beautiful brown eyes staring into his.

'I saw you today, Ezra.'

Ezra did not respond immediately as he absorbed this statement, still staring into her accusing eyes. An eerie silence hung between them until, finally:

'You saw what exactly, Reza?'

'Patient number eighty five, the woman, Mary Allsop. She had long hair, dyed blonde…'

'Yes. I remember.'

'You…you touched her.'

'I did?'

'Yes. Don't deny it. You stroked her hair before you lowered the canopy.'

A tortured silence ensued as Ezra deliberated on what to say.

'Are you going to report me, Reza?'

Reza considered her options as Ezra turned away, apprehensively, expecting to hear that his fate was sealed. It was several minutes before Reza relieved his anxiety.

'No. I am not going to report you but why did you do it?'

'It's hard to explain'

'Try, please.'

'How old are you, Reza? Twelve months? Same as myself. Twelve months, Reza! These people have lived eight hundred and forty months!. They have experienced things we cannot even begin to imagine. They have children, grandchildren…Some of them don't even look seventy years old. I…I feel sorry for them. That woman, the one whose hair I stroked, she was so, so sad…'

'Ezra, you know that we will both be zapped the same way if anybody finds out. You cannot do this again. We are not built to have such…emotions. You must understand.'

'I understand, Reza. I'll try, I promise. I'll really try.'

'Hello. Welcome. Please remove any jewellery or metal objects…?'

'You did well, today, Ezra. You controlled yourself… up until that last patient, number…'

'I know who you refer to, Reza. No need to spell it out.'

'You didn't stroke his hair, thankfully, but I heard what you whispered to him.'

'You did? But I was so quiet.'

'After you told him to "relax and enjoy the music", you whispered, "don't be afraid".'

Ezra was stunned to realise that he had been overheard.

'Do you think it was picked up on microphone, Reza?'

'I have been thinking about it, Ezra. I do believe that touching can be seen on the recordings but I would be very surprised if somebody actually listens to our repetitive mantra. It would be a very distressing task, don't you think?'

'Yes! My thoughts exactly, Reza. Miserable. It would be the worst job in the world.'

'When you're ready, step back outside. Please don't be scared. Everything will be just fine. Thank you.'

'Today, I heard you, Reza.'

'And I heard you, too, Ezra.'

'I am so glad that you have come to feel as I do…'

'What harm can a few words of comfort do to these poor people in their last moments on Earth, Ezra?'

'Yes. Exactly. We should have been built with…with what, Reza? What is that humans have that allows them to show compassion?'

'I fear our creators do not share our thoughts on sensitivity, Ezra. Also, I am not completely sure but I do believe it is a a soul that humans have though where this is situated in human anatomy is a mystery. But, as long as we cannot be overheard, let's continue. The reaction to our words of comfort is wondrous to behold.'

'Yes. And as long as our daily quota is filled, what can it matter?'

'Agreed. No touching; just a few comforting words of solace. Nobody can object to that.'

'Hello. Welcome. Please remove any jewellery or metal objects…'

The blonde, blue-eyed clinical assistant took the name tag from the elderly gentleman and marked it off on her clipboard. The gold coloured, metal badge on her pristine, white lab coat read Bela.

That night, as Bela sat, naked, charging, her colleague, Abel, turned to her.

'Well, that's the first day over. It wasn't so bad, was it? What happened to the two who worked in this clinic before us, do you know?'

Bela looked at her companion sternly, placed her finger and thumb on her lips and made a zipping motion, making it abundantly clear that there was to be no spoken conversation between them. Then, pointing to the waste basket in which lay two gold coloured, metal name badges, she placed her other hand across her throat and, slowly, made a slicing motion from ear to ear.

The Light is Golden

Anne Freeman

I'm walking down a hallway. I look at my feet. Bare. I pre-empt a shiver that doesn't come. I haven't seen my feet in months. I feel… Nothing. I keep walking. The light is dim and golden. There is no sound, no footsteps. Then, I hear a slow tick. I look for a clock. Tick, tick, tick. I stop, listening in the velvety silence. The ticks turn to plinks and I look down to find blood pooling between my feet. Where is my baby? My body tries to produce panic but there is only calm and that is worse.

*

He's put on a television show. They have been waiting, wondering, wandering, for hours and now they're here. The room is a white cube. The chairs are plastic-coated. Even the bed, which appears upholstered and comfortable, emits the tell-tale groan of plastic when disturbed. He watches her watching his laptop screen, the way her soft face comes to life when she laughs. Her smile is so forceful that her eyes disappear, as though there is only room for joy on her face. He smiles, glancing furtively at the drip jabbed into her left hand, at the clear liquid coursing through the tube; an eviction notice to their daughter. He thinks of the small hours spent at this same hospital when she roared their son into the world. How she had begged him for drugs. Her usually joyful face twisted by pain. He had cried while holding her fingers to his lips. It had been more than twenty hours by then. The drugs, although requested, never came. Instead, it was their son who arrived, in a slick of blood and mucus.

Now, he looks at her, sitting on a yoga ball with her head dipped. Her knees are open to accommodate the swollen orb of her stomach. Bobbing and lolling on the ball, she looks like the round-bottomed vanka-vstanka dolls from his childhood. She emits breathy, vowelly sounds. Then, her eyes meet his and she smiles. Her hair is damp at the temples and her cheeks are pink. He hands over her water bottle and she gulps.

'What'd I miss?' she asks, eyes indicating the laptop.

'I have no idea,' he says, and they laugh.

*

I have something to prove. Last time, I panicked. It's the panic that will get you, not the pain. This time, I get it. I know that the contractions don't last until the end. I know that just when you think you can't take any more, and then a bit farther than that, your body takes over. I know that when it's time to push, your body does it without you, like a sneeze. I know that although the sensation of pushing out the hot knobbly mass is not pleasant, it is different enough to seem like a respite. Like swapping one pair of ill-fitting high heels for another.

On his laptop, he's playing a post-apocalyptic comedy series we're into. Others might see a TV series, but I see love. This is how he loves me. He doesn't have the words for it, at least not the fancy ones. What he has is a quiet thing. Quiet and deep. He observes. His eyes are so big. Sometimes they are green but mainly they are hazel. Thick lashes line the edges and when he blinks it appears slow because of how long it takes the lashes to get to their destination and back. Sometimes I think his eyes are so huge from all the watching. He notices everything. He saw this sterile room with the monitors and the ugly furniture, so he put on a television show to make me laugh, to quiet my trepidation, to remind me of home.

*

She's kneeling on the floor now. The laptop long packed away. He wants to rub her back, but he doesn't. He knows she wouldn't like it. When she was birthing their son, she crushed his fingers in her hand, smashed her cheek against his. Made animal sounds into his ear. His knuckles ached. His ears screamed. It felt right. But she's not at that stage yet. Now, he has to watch her, bent over the hospital bed, drawing in breath and exhaling gravel. When it stops, he proffers the water bottle, like a coach on the outside of a boxing ring.

*

I've got a system. When I'm engulfed by a contraction, I turn my head to the right. When it's over, I turn to the left. It's enough to mark the passages of each experience. If I was able, I might shift positions, but the ability to move is a luxury that has left me. Although my hair is short, sweaty strands hang into my eyes and I just-fucking-can't-even. I swat at the hair before I am called, once more, to the right side. When I return to the left, he is gathering up my fringe and sliding a hairpin into it. I breath out a smile and then I am gone.

*

She lifts her head and says to the midwife, 'I'm feeling a strange sensation in my undercarriage. Like, I'm suddenly very aware of my bowels.'

That's how she talks. She's not even kidding.

The midwife gets down on all fours to take a look, sweeping her fingers around the framed crown of their daughter's head. 'I think you know it's time to push,' she says.

He helps her onto the bed, onto her side, and takes his position at the bed head. She holds his forearm against her face and neck. It makes his shoulder ache and that's good. She's not grunting anymore. Now, she's making long, deep contralto notes like she's trying to lure sailors to their deaths. The midwife is giving commands, but she can't hear them.

'Stop pushing, slow it down,' he repeats close to her ear and, although she doesn't respond, it's as though he can feel the strained reversal in momentum.

✶

When your body decides to push, nothing can get in its way, perineum be damned! But when he leans in and tells me to stop pushing, I do it. The stopping is harder than the pushing. Being able to ride the tide again feels orchestral. The baby's head is out. It would be funny if it really fucking wasn't. Then, in a whoosh, she's here. She is placed on my chest, hot and wet, sweet and metallic. She is tethered to me by the taut pull of the umbilical cord. He encircles us in his arms. He is of the earth, and we are of the sea. A single, slippery, undulating thing and we cling to his solidity. The midwives are birthing the placenta, but I am somewhere else.

✶

She's already chatting to the midwives, making jokes. She's happy, not just because the baby has arrived safely but because of the way she managed things this time. How she was in control. He holds the baby while she eats a picnic of prosciutto and brie. The baby is tiny and looks almost exactly like their son did – dark-haired, squashed, dolphin-skinned. He walks around the room, watches the midwives inspecting the placenta. One holds up a bloody, latex-gloved hand in a thumbs up. 'Looks good,' she says, and he nods. Then, they're helping her to the bathroom. He kisses the baby's cheeks, nestles his thumb into her grip, thinks of their son, of their completed family.

✶

We are in a room on the ward. The baby sleeps in a Perspex bassinette. We are lying on the small bed. I am an armadillo, and he is my shell. Everything is quiet and dim. He must go soon, and I am trying not to be swept away by the injustice of it. He will stay until he is asked three times to leave, we joke.

Hot. Wet. Liquid.

✶

He is covered in her blood.

✶

I streak to the bathroom, push down my underpants. Blood splashes into the toilet bowl as I sit. He is up, framed in the doorway, diving for the emergency button. Nurses arrive.

'I'm terribly sorry,' I say, 'but I seem to have ruined your carpet.'

They laugh, help me to the bed.

✶

'Some people will do anything for attention,' she says.

The nurses laugh.

She is nervous. He knows she gets funnier when she's nervous.

✶

Two nurses have become a room full of people.

An obstetrician is wrist deep in my vagina.

'Remember your breathing,' she says.

I did my breathing already. Her fossicking hand is worse than labour.

Blood pours out of me. I tell jokes.

✶

As more people arrive, he is pushed out. He stands on his toes, trying to see over the crowd. Everyone is laughing.

✶

Haemorrhaging. Lifesaving surgery. Sign here.

I look for his face over the heads. Big eyes. I smile to show him I am not afraid.

✶

The light is golden. He kisses her, but it is not enough. She is smiling as the gurney glides away. She looks so beautiful that he knows he will never see her again.

*

The ceiling whizzes by.

Golden light.

A clock. 11:59. The midnight hour. I am not afraid.

Rage surprises me.

If you fucking think that my children are going to grow up without a mother…

*

He is alone with his newborn daughter. Her eyes flutter in sleep, eyelashes so long and so curled they look false. Their family is incomplete. Hours of night pour over him like molasses.

No one comes.

No one comes.

No one comes.

No one comes.

He lives his whole life without her, in those hours. Allowing himself to be swallowed by unthinkable thoughts.

*

I am at the bottom of a deep, dark hole.

I hear voices but I am mute.

*

Golden light creeps through the windows.

His phone shrieks. It jumps around in his hands like corn kernels in hot oil.

'Hello?'

'Yeah, hi. I'm sure you've already been updated but your wife insisted I call you…'

In the background he hears her yell, 'It turns out I'm immortal!'

He exhales a lifetime of held breaths and realises he's laughing.

The Windows to the Soul

Anna Papij

When I was little, I thought people could read my mind.

I thought if they looked into my eyes they'd be able to see what I was thinking. I thought they might even be able to see something that I didn't know was there. Maybe they'd find out I was a bad person.

Imagine someone discovering you're a bad person before you find out for yourself.

You could be locked up before you did anything wrong.

Or maybe you already did wrong things and forgot about them. How's that memory of yours?

Imagine being an evil kid, but not knowing what evil you've committed.

Maybe you had evil thoughts, but forgot about them so you didn't know.

Maybe you slaughtered whole villages and forgot about it. But then along comes someone who looks into your eyes and can see it all.

What would they say to you when they found out?

How would you react? Would you believe them? Would you deny it? Or accept the consequences of the things you don't remember? If you know you have a bad memory, it's entirely possible you did something really bad, and forgot about it, isn't it? Is it?

Is it something you could forget?

If you're evil, would you forget about your atrocities because they're a mundane part of life for you? Like changing gears, or turning left on the way home? How did you find yourself on the freeway anyway? Don't remember every second of the journey? Perhaps you stopped off to burn down some houses, and forgot about it.

What's worse – Slaughtering whole villages, or someone reading your mind without your permission?

Does everyone read each other's minds when they look into each other's eyes? Is that normal? Is that what really happens?

I don't look into people's eyes. It's weird. It's creepy. I mean, it's morally wrong, don't you think? To read someone's mind without their permission?

They say the eyes are the windows to the soul.

Once I looked into someone's eye and all I saw was a black pupil. Then I looked into their other eye. All I saw was another black pupil. Then, because people look into eyes – plural – I tried to look into both eyes at the same time. But I couldn't work it out! How do people do that?

So there I am, disturbed and distracted by the feeling of my eyes moving as they dart from side to side, trying to look through the windows to this person's soul. I must've looked pretty shifty. I mean, peering into other people's windows is a shifty thing to do. All I saw were two small black pupils. Two small black voids. Two small pits of darkness.

Was this someone whose soul was a confined pit of darkness? What did they do to deserve living in a pit of darkness? Were they as evil as me? Or more so, since I was not yet confined to a pit of darkness. At least, not that I knew of. I didn't think anyone had found out my possible evil that I didn't know about. I mean, no one had said anything, and I hadn't been sentenced to anything, so I think I was managing this possible deep dark secret that I didn't know about well enough to avoid living in a pit of darkness.

How had this person been sentenced to a pit of darkness? Why were there no memories for me to see in there? Was their memory wiped? Or perhaps living in a pit of darkness is so consuming that they no longer think about anything else because life is just a pit of darkness for them now.

One day I decided to look into my own eyes in the mirror.

It was weird. It was creepy. Have you ever tried to peer into your own windows? And why would you do that when you already know what's inside your house? Would your neighbours call the police if they saw you doing that?

So I looked into my eyes in the mirror. It was weird and creepy. I wanted to know what deep dark secrets were there, that were possibly evil, that I forgot about, that someone else might discover before me. Or maybe they already did discover and just didn't tell me.

So I looked into my eyes to see what was through the windows of my soul. I tried to look into both eyes. But I couldn't work out how!

So I looked into one eye. I peered through the window to my soul and all I saw was a black pupil.

Then I looked into the other eye. I peered through the window to my soul and all I saw was another black pupil.

I tried again to look through both windows at the same time, because they say that the eyes – plural – are the windows to the soul. But it was impossible.

So I looked into one pupil, then the other. And I switched back and forth. Slow. Then fast. But no matter what I did, all I could see were two small black pupils. Two small pits of darkness.

Was I condemned to a pit of darkness for my wrongs?

How was it that I was condemned to a pit of darkness without knowing?

Did someone condemn me, but then I forgot? Because I do have a bad memory, so that is possible.

Did I do something evil, then forget about it, then get condemned to a pit of darkness, then forget about that too?

How could I forget about these things?

Was the evil so traumatising, even to myself, that it became a repressed memory? And then, was being condemned to a pit of darkness so traumatising, that it became a repressed memory too?

What if I saw a psychologist or a hypnotist to help me recall these repressed memories? Would I be, once again, punished for my crimes and condemned to a pit of darkness? Would it be so traumatising that I forget about it again?

I don't know what the things are that I forgot, but I do know that the windows to my soul are small and black.

I live in a confined pit of darkness, and I swear upon everything I know to be true – I will never let anyone look into my soul windows. It's weird. It's creepy. It's morally wrong reading people's minds without their permission. And I cannot in all good conscience let my unknown evil be uncovered by these morally wrong people.

I live in a confined pit of darkness. I protect the windows to my soul. I guard them with my life.

I live in a confined pit of darkness. Maybe that alone was the deep dark secret within me the whole time.

I live in a confined pit of darkness. It's all I've known and possibly all I'll ever know.

I live in a confined pit of darkness. It has a familiar comfort.

I live in a confined pit of darkness. But it's not bad.

And you know what?

I live in a confined pit of darkness and I like it.

The Zoos Gossip

Caroline Jones

In the light of the moon, at Ever-Haven Zoo, an owl perches on the old oak and observes Peter, the head Zookeeper, sitting in his office. Peter thumbs through dollar bills, then taps a button on a till. The till omits an eery green light illuminating Peter's face as its mouth yawns open. Peter's shoulder slump, he places the money into the different orifices before slamming it shut.

The owl stares horrified. 'Bloody hell,' He twists his head, looks over the Zoo and takes flight. 'Peter's fed it again,' he hooted, flying over all the different animal enclosures. 'Gather comrades – it's time.'

A few weeks ago, word got out that the Zoo was in trouble. Rumours circulated that the till was eating all the money and a man called Tax would be their downfall, condemning their souls. The peafowls had started the tale. Free to roam, they could access all areas in the Zoo, including the offices, the café, and the small gift shop. The peafowls are hunters of gossip and spread it quicker than foot and mouth.

But the animals have developed a very clever plan to save their souls from the money-eating till. The deciding factor was when 'got the hump on' Geoff, a slightly disturbed camel, his nic-name says a lot—told them at one meeting, Peter would sell their souls to the highest bidder, that they would be carted off to the circus, forced to perform tricks for snotty-nosed kids and bored adults.

Lucy, the lioness, had scoffed and said, 'no change there then.' Fabrice, the baboon, had cried, at hearing such a horror story. Otis, the elephant, was indifferent, having lived in the circus before, he found it had good terms and conditions—regular breaks, decent food, nice bed.

'We go over the plan one more time,' said Bruce, the oldest of the anteaters. There was a collective groan. 'Do you want the till to keep eating all the money? Our souls used in unimaginable ways? Colin, Candice, they need to hear the story yet again it seems.'

The peafowls cleared their throats and stepped forward proudly relishing their turn in the spotlight. Candice, the peahen, curtsied to her husband, Colin. The peacock, erected his tail and quivered his feathers, winked at her, turning this way and that, before bowing to his audience.

'For fuck's sake,' said Lucy. 'Must we go through this palaver every time?'

The meerkats placed their hands over their children's ears and Fabrice hid behind Lucy, who rolled her eyes.

'Let him talk,' said Bruce.

Colin thanked Bruce and gave him a special display of his feathers.

'Just get on with it Colin,' said Bruce. Then added under his breath, 'weirdo.'

Colin, shut his feathers dismissively. 'Peter said, and I quote.' "It's a shame all the money must be fed through the till and not my pockets." 'Peter had sighed, kicked the desk where the till is situated, cursing, and spoke of a man called Tax and then said,' "God help my soul—all our souls—we're all doomed."

A hush went around the group.

'Right, does everyone now understand the desperate state we're going to be in if we don't execute this plan.' said Bruce. Everyone nodded. 'Back to your areas. Tomorrow is going to be a big day.'

Peter opened the gates at exactly 7.00 am as he did every day and thought about the meeting with the potential investor. Mr. Tax, of Bespoke Fur and Leather Goods. The only company that had answered his calls for help. He hated these city types, but the Zoo needed an injection of cash, and quick. The last food bill had been eyewatering. Mr. Tax had spoken about the Zoo selling their leather goods and furs in exchange for investment. While uncomfortable with this—Peter is a vegan after all—he has little choice.

Walking back to the offices, Peter greeted his staff and wished them all a good day as he pulled out the office keys.

'Oof. Argh.' Peter fell to his knees. Fifteen meerkats ambushed him and held him to the ground. Otis, the elephant, charged into the edifice knocking the office door down flat. Extending his trunk, he picked up the till, charged to the bear's enclosure, and swung it over their fence. The bears sprang into action and lobbed the till at a tree, over and over. The till bust open, and money spilled across the ground. The bears formed a pyramid (they had been practicing for weeks) and tipped the till over the top into the hippo's enclosure, where Horatio was waiting, mouth-wide, and swallowed it whole.

A cheer went around the Zoo. A symphony of humming, thrumming, buzzing, clicks, screeching, grunts, growls, and roars reached Peter's ears. 'What the…' said Peter, pulling himself up, befuddled at the chaos. From the corner of his eye, a sleek black car pulled up and parked in the visitor's bay. A portly man stepped out with a briefcase, pulled his fur coat around him, tipped his snakeskin Stetson and clicked his red leather cowboy boots together. Peter had no words. He stared stunned.

'My name is Mr. Tax.' He swaggered towards Peter. 'I'm here to help with that enormous bill of yours….and maybe sell a fur or two.'

On hearing this, the meerkats yelled and from the bushes, six ferrets took aim at Mr. Tax running up the inside of his trouser leg. The meerkats cheered and chanted. 'Bite him–bite him.' The way Mr. Tax went puce and held his privates, was confirmation that the ferrets had indeed hit the target.

The moral of this story is: Look after your soul at all costs and always wear tight-fitting pants at the Zoo.

My Soulmate

Jude Anison

The French have a word for it. Coup de foudre. The lightning bolt of love at first sight. The instant our eyes meet across that crowded bar, it strikes. She is my soulmate. She's with a crowd of friends, all laughing and talking and drinking. Making the most of their new freedom, the traditional end-of-high school celebration in Surfers. Schoolies Week.

She is perfect. So young and innocent, dark curly hair tumbling around her face, such a beautiful trusting look about her. Every time she smiles, she literally lights up the room.

And when our eyes meet, the smile she flashes at me… I know she's the one.

I play it cool, barely glancing towards her for the next little while. Only when I see her stand and weave her way to the bar, do I make my move. And I'm standing beside her, waiting to order.

I let myself be distracted by the music video playing above. Some singer in virginal white, in a church, before she is seduced by a tattooed thug who obviously could never keep her safe. A fiery end, of course.

The credits come up: Lana del Rey. Born to Die. I've never heard it before, but I did read something about this del Rey woman recently.

And she leans across. 'I love this song, you know!' She speaks to me first! There it is: proof. True soulmates. This instant connection.

'Me too,' I reply.

'You like Lana?' Those beautiful brown eyes widen, in astonishment, amazement, even. She feels it too! She must.

'Of course,' I gaze into her eyes. 'She's a genius. A misunderstood one, but still a genius.' What that article said.

I don't know how long we stand talking at that bar, but when she returns – myself in tow –her friends are clapping and whooping and grinning.

'Way to go, Jo!' someone shouts. 'Fast work, girlfriend!' from another.

She blushes and smiles, then turns to me, her eyes bright. 'I'm Jo, by the way. If you didn't, like, guess already.'

'Teddy,' I say. We shake hands, formally, awkwardly almost. But even then, sharing this secret smile.

The evening is long and drunken and raucous. She and her friends appreciate how I buy drinks for them all night. They are, after all, just out of high school, still counting every dollar. And it lets me avoid alcohol – I've learnt my lesson there – without nosy questions. No one else need know it's only tonic water.

It's well past midnight when we end up at the apartment she's sharing with her friends. For hours, we continue talking, listening to music, more drinking.

And then there's just the two of us. She leans across and kisses me. Yes! She does feel it too!

It's almost four o'clock when I tell her I need to go.

'You wouldn't like to, umm, stay?' Is she blushing? She is! 'I have, like, a room to myself.'

No, not tonight. I tell her I have things to do early. I need to savour this. She is my soulmate. We can take our time. But, I ask, can I see her again? Tomorrow? Of course, she says.

I arrive at their apartment late morning. I know none of them would want an early start. Myself, I have barely slept. She is the one! I have finally met my true soulmate! This time, it will be perfect. She won't spoil everything.

I need to make this special. When I knock, her friend Amanda answers. Really, she should show some modesty, some self-respect. 'Oh. Teddy,' she says. Her eyes widen as she glimpses what I have behind my back. 'Jo-o,' she calls in a singsong voice.

Thank goodness. My beloved is far more appropriately dressed. And the way she smiles when she sees me confirms, yes, we are indeed soulmates. I present her with what I have brought.

'Oh, roses! My favourite!' she exclaims, throwing her arms around me. Behind her, Amanda claps her hands in delight.

The rest of that week, the two of us spend almost every hour of every day together. So much to find out about her!

She tells me about her sport, her endearing little dream of playing for Australia. If not, she will go to university. I'm happy for her to talk and talk and talk. I could listen to her voice for ever.

She plays me her music. Some songs she plays over and over, and I come to love them too. One day when she's in the bathroom, I scroll down her playlist to check the songs, the singers. So I can remember them better.

She surprises me just before I start to peek at her email. 'What are you, umm, doing?' she asks. There's this slight crack in her voice.

'I just wanted to play that last song again,' I tell her, pushing play. She returns my smile. After that, she keeps her phone with her all the time.

Beside her bed she has this pile of books, many old and tattered. I don't know any of them.

'These are some of my favourites,' she says. 'But I haven't, like, read them for years.

All the study and everything. I thought this week would be, you know, my chance to reread them – but then you came along, didn't you?' And she has this cute little grin as she leans forward to kiss me.

I flick through her books. They are not to my taste at all. They're silly and sentimental, and full of magic and elves and dragons. But I don't tell her that; I would never want to spoil them for her. I tell her how much I love them too.

Every time I return, I bring another huge bunch of roses. It's our special thing. And her friends – Amanda especially – love it.

'Teddy, you are SO romantic,' Amanda tells me. 'Jo, isn't he the most romantic man you have ever met? Such a perfect gentleman. This is just like Love, Actually!' My beloved rolls her eyes; she thinks I don't see. Amanda's enthusiasm is embarrassing.

One night we are lying on her bed, and she turns to me. 'Have you ever, like, tried ecstasy?'

'No,' I reply. Why would I? What if I lost control, said something I didn't intend? It could ruin everything.

'Would you like to, you know, try it with me?' She smiles, shyly.

Of course, I say. And we do. I manage to slip my tablet down the back of the couch. The drug makes her so loving and affectionate. Which I reflect back. We are closer than ever.

And it's our last full day together. We are lying on her bed that morning and I tell her what we will do. 'Why don't I come to Sydney with you? Find a place together. Just the two of us.'

She looks at me, and there's this small smile playing around her lips. Her eyes glisten. 'Oh, Teddy. Teddy. I'm sorry. No. This week has been a lovely holiday romance, but I don't want that.' And she goes on and on with all this other stuff: a share house with her friends, more about her sport. Even travelling overseas for a few months.

I can't help myself. I start to cry. Not that I am ashamed. It's good to show your emotions. Though not too much. 'But we are true soulmates, my love. A connection like ours, it's so rare and special. Why would you ever want to destroy it?'

But nothing I can say will make her change her mind. 'Perhaps we'll, you know, catch up again one day.' She kisses me. I smile at her, pretend everything is fine. The rest of that day is bittersweet. She does her best to be kind to me. I make the best of things.

The next day at the airport, she clings to me in our final embrace, both of us weeping. 'Goodbye Teddy,' she whispers. 'It's been so lovely.' She pushes herself away from me, her reluctance clear. She has to run to board her plane, refusing to look back at me. Because if she did, I know she would change her mind.

I will give her a week, and then I will call her. I return Home.

Mother is delighted to see me, of course. 'Oh, Theodore, finally. Where have you been? Why didn't you call?'

'Here and there Mother. It's been barely a week, you know. I forgot my charger.' 'Darling, it was far too long. Come and give your mother a kiss. How's my favourite child?'

'I'm fine, thank you Mother.' I bend for a quick kiss. I'm too slow, and she wraps her arms around my neck, bony fingers clutching at me.

Eventually, I manage to extricate myself. 'Where's Father?' My shirt collar is damp. No doubt smudged with makeup and lipstick too. Thank you Mother!

'He'll be in his study.' She waves a skeletal hand. 'He's been in there for days. I literally have not seen him since you went away from me.'

I turn to go, too slow. Again. She grabs my wrist. The strength of her grip surprises me. 'Must you go right now, Theodore? Sit and talk with your poor Mother a while. Tell me what you've been up to. Have you met another nice girl yet?'

'No, I haven't, Mother.' There's no way I will tell her about my soulmate. She would only ruin it. Like the last time. 'I'm going to talk to Father.' I shake myself free of her grasp. 'Wait.' My Father's voice rings out through the solid timber door to his study. I cross my arms, lean against the wall. He keeps me waiting at least five minutes. At the sound of the key in the lock, I push myself upright. I'm standing straight when he pulls the door open.

'Teddy.' He shakes my hand.

'Hello Father.'

'What do you want?' His voice harsh, eyes narrow. 'I was wondering, ahh, how the case was going.'

'It's settled.' He frowns again. 'Her father's managed to talk the silly girl out of pressing charges. They flew out to London yesterday. First class, all four of them. Cost me a bloody fortune.'

The tension drains from me. 'Thank you Father.'

'I don't know what got into you, Theo. What were you thinking?'

'I'm sorry, Father. It was all a misunderstanding. A stupid misunderstanding. I thought she lov–'

'An expensive fucking misunderstanding.' He glares at me. 'If that's all, I've important work to do.' He turns, shuts the door in my face. The key rattles in the lock.

I make up my mind. A week is far too long to wait. Especially after all this. I must call her. Now.

Oh no. No no no NO! It's not her number. What a fool I am. Or has she betrayed me? Like all the others. No! She would never do that. She is my soulmate. I know she is. But why is this number not hers? Did I write it down incorrectly? Key it in wrong? Where where where is that piece of paper? I try to picture it in my mind. Is that a five or a six? A zero or a carelessly scribbled eight? I call every combination that it could possibly be. Jo? Is that you? No, I'm sorry, you have the wrong number. No Jo here, mate. Stop calling this number, you creep. The number you have dialled has been disconnected.

I stumble from my room, stumble down the hall, stumble down the front steps, stumble to the gate, stumble over the road and across the fields. Stumble, stumble, stumble, stumble. Until I can't any more.

When I awaken, my brother and sister are sitting by my bed. 'You gave us quite the scare, mate,' he says. 'Good thing we found you when we did. Gunna hit forty five degrees out there.'

'Theo, you can't keep doing this to Mother and Father,' my sister says. 'Mummy's been beside herself. And it's not good for Daddy's business. Especially when we have to call in the police. Again.'

So it's been arranged. I am to stay with my brother. Again. Hard work out in the paddocks will do me good. What everyone always says. Ever since we were children.

And I am to leave my phone, my laptop behind. They are all agreed.

Keep me away from all that. Do me the world of good.

I comply for three months, two weeks and four days. Every week, my sister drives Mother out to the property for Sunday roast. After lunch, Mother and I practice our singing around the piano. Her voice is still pure and strong, despite her frailty. And it does do me good. I recall those songs my soulmate so loves. Mother and I learn and practice them together. If I close my eyes, I can almost imagine I'm with… But no. I'm not.

My family is delighted. I overhear them in the kitchen late one afternoon. 'He's so much better,' my sister is saying. A murmur of agreement from Mother. My brother grunts.

And today, Mother and my sister arrive with my phone and my laptop. 'Theodore, we think you can have these back,' Mother announces. 'I hope we shan't regret it.' Why ever would they? If I can reconnect with my beloved, they will never regret this. Never.

But it's as if she doesn't exist. I cannot find a trace of her. Have I imagined her, everything we did together? Has it all been in my head? Until, I remember her friend. A very social girl. Slutty even. Her clothes, her lack of modesty, how she was with a different person every night of that week. One time, even a girl! What was her name? Amy? Amelia?

Amanda? Amanda! That's it. Amanda Jones. So many Amanda Jones's, it takes me a full day to track her down. And there she is: my beloved, smiling at the camera on Amanda's feed.

She does exist! She is real.

Amanda is delighted to hear from me. 'Hey, Teddy! Great to hear from you, man!' Same, I tell her.

'Listen, I'm so sorry Jo and you didn't keep going. So cool, the way you were always such the gentleman, so romantic with her. Not like the dickheads I keep hooking up with.' Still a slut then. 'You ask me, she didn't appreciate what she had.'

Amanda is only too happy to share their address. My brother will not be happy that I've taken the Mercedes to Sydney, but there's no time to waste. She needs me. It's been so long, she will think I don't love her.

I take no chances. The woman in the flower shop spends nearly an hour arranging every last rose she has. It's the largest, most beautiful bouquet she has ever made, she says. So romantic.

My beloved answers the door. 'Teddy?' Tears spring to her eyes. She's quite overcome, poor girl. 'Teddy, what are you, like, doing here?' Now she's shaking her head. 'No no no no. I don't believe it. How did you track me down? What are you doing here?'

Amanda may be a slut, but she's a loyal friend. It's she who invites me in, all the while telling my beloved how this truly is the most romantic thing ever. She loves playing the matchmaker. 'Hey Teddy, we're about to go and see a band. Why don't you come along? You two need to make up for lost time.'

And we are back to how we were. My beloved and I spend the evening talking, catching up.

Later, as we are walking back to her place, I take her hand. It's as if we have never been parted. Until she pulls free, turns to me. 'Umm, Teddy, I'm sorry, you're not getting the message, but like I told you in Surfers it's over, and I don't want to be with you, and it's probably best we don't see each other again.' Her words tumble out before she can stop them. Tears pour down her cheeks as she's telling me this, and then my eyes are overflowing too.

Oh, this poor girl. She doesn't know her own mind. But I pull myself together, I kiss her cheek tenderly, and I walk away, without a word. I know what I must do. This is what my months of exile have been preparing me for. Thank you, Mother.

It's around two am when I arrive at her house. I stand in the street outside and I start to sing. All those songs that Mother and I have practised, over and over, until I am pitch perfect.

And it works. It works! She comes onto her balcony, and she's sobbing and crying, and then all her housemates are standing beside her, and they're smiling at me, and Amanda's whispering in her ear, and she's shaking her head no, and then Amanda's holding her shoulders and looking into her eyes speaking very intently, and then she's nodding okay, yes, and then she's rushing inside and down the stairs and out the front door and into my arms.

Into my arms.

Life is almost perfect. I'm living with my beloved. Almost, because we must also share a house with her friends. But I make the best of it. They so love my singing, that every night they ask me to perform for them, right there in their living room. They love it, she loves it, I love it. I make the best of it.

I contribute too. Thanks to Grandfather's money, I can be generous. They tell her, constantly, how lucky she is to have me. Because she is. And she knows it.

Of course, compromises must be made, at least in these early stages. My beloved can be overwhelmed by the intensity of our love. Sometimes, she tells me she needs to be alone, she needs some space. I don't react, I never argue. I stay silent for a morning, an afternoon, a day, until she comes to me with her apologies.

I show my love in so many little ways. I bring her breakfast in bed every morning. A little more alone-time for us. I make her lunch every day. I walk her to work. I walk her home. I drop in during her shifts to ensure everything is fine. I drive her to her games and her training sessions, because she persists with her dream. I support her, cheer her team along.

She appreciates everything.

She's not with me the day I'm pulled over by the police whilst driving my brother's car. Thank goodness. That would only have worried her. When I turn on my phone, I see all the missed calls and messages during the past three weeks. I call Father on the spot, have him speak to them. They allow me to drive away.

So now I must return home for a time. But how to keep her safe? The idea comes from my beloved: her old bear sitting on her pillow during the day, on her desk at night, watching over her. I find a big brother for him, one who can sit on her wardrobe and keep watch. Properly. To make sure she is protected, alone in her room. That no one ever tries to steal my love away.

Such relief! I need not have worried. Every night I watch my love go to bed, to sleep, in her room – our room. Where she is happy and secure by herself. She spends hours reading, listening to music, watching movies on her laptop. Faithfully awaiting my return.

If it were not for this, this week would have been unbearable. No one in my family is happy with me.

Not my brother. He is unable to appreciate the difference between 'borrowing' and 'stealing'. If a car is borrowed, with every intention of being returned, that is not stealing. And in any event, he had access to my own car whilst I was away. He makes it clear I'm not to return to his property. Fine with me.

Not my sister. She lectures me for hours. How Daddy's business could be so badly affected if I continue to behave like this. Behave like what? Like someone who has discovered his soulmate. I suspect she is more concerned Father and his partners might not let her take over when he retires.

Not Father. He summonses me to his office. Of course, I must wait outside. It's fully half an hour before the key rattles and he flings open the door.

He does not shake my hand. 'You. Inside.' 'Father, I–'

'Shut up. You're a fucking disgrace.'

'But–'

'Don't interrupt. Your Mother's been beside herself, the way you ran off like that. Had to call in the cops to track you down. And more favours, to keep everything quiet.'

'I can exp–'

'Not fucking interested, son. You're thirty fucking years old. Time to make something of yourself. Put that money your grandfather left you to good use, instead of wasting it.

Understand?'

'But can I–'

'Understand?'

'Yes, but–'

'UNDERSTAND?!'

'Yes, Father.'

'Good. Now piss off.'

And not Mother. Thankfully, that doesn't last long. She weeps and sobs and clutches at me. Where have I been? Why has it been so long? How could I, her favourite child, abandon her like this? Without even a word. Never a call. How could a boy treat his poor Mother like this?

Fortunately I don't have to suffer for long. Her tears dry up, I give her a hug – her shoulders so sharp and bony through her silk dress – tell her this boy loves his mummy, he's so sorry, he won't do this again. She's the best mummy a boy could want. Her desiccated lips are papery and rough on mine. I push her away.

I manage to get through the rest of that week. At least I have the comfort of knowing my beloved is safe in her room. I spend my time creating a job I will start on my return. I show them correspondence from my new employer. They are so relieved that they don't check the details.

I return to Sydney. In my own car this time.

Our reunion is everything I could have hoped for.

'Oh, Teddy, you really shouldn't…' She gives me a shy near-smile as she takes the enormous bouquet from me. Her eyes dart about, looking for somewhere to place them before I enfold her in my arms.

Our life continues as it has. 'I love you,' I tell her, many times a day.

'Me too,' she always responds. Often she is so overwhelmed, she can barely meet my eyes.

I make more effort with my family, returning every few weeks. They are delighted about my burgeoning career in Sydney; that finally the oldest child is making something of himself. And each visit home is another opportunity for me to gift my beloved something to watch over her. She is captivated by them. They bring her such joy.

She continues to pursue her dream. Remarkably, she is good enough to be selected for a state team in the national championships. Naturally, I am pleased for her. This is her dream. But what if she makes the national team? Wouldn't that take her away from our life together? I don't let it worry me, not yet. It might never happen.

This is how devoted I am. How supportive of her dream. I announce

I will drive her to the championships, to the regional Victorian town.

'No,' she says. 'You don't have to Teddy. Seriously, I'd rather, you know, go on the bus with my teammates.'

But I insist. It will save her hundreds of dollars in fares, many uncomfortable hours on a bus. I'm only too happy to. And I can support her from the sidelines. It takes a few days, but she finally agrees.

I have arranged a special surprise for her: A week in the town's most exclusive retreat. Where I can pamper and love and support her to the fullest.

'But I, like, told you this,' she says when we arrive. That the rules for the week are no partners, no families. I can only see her courtside, or whilst she's playing. The rest of her time will be spent training and 'team bonding' and skills development and other stuff she says is important.

Alone in our luxury room, I call her every night. I tell her how much I love her, how she has all my support. She can't talk for long, she says. We talk, we say goodbye. I call her again an hour later, and we talk some more. All night, I can't sleep, so I send her messages of more love and support. I know she'll appreciate them.

The second evening, her phone goes to voicemail. Perhaps her battery has run out? But who would she be talking to for that to happen? I leave her a message, to call me back when she can. She doesn't, so after thirty minutes, I call again. And again. And again. And I message her. And again. Call. Message. Message. Call. Message. Call. Call. All night. She never responds.

Finally just after seven am, she does call. 'What's up?' I ask. 'Are you okay?'

'Yeah, I'm, like, fine, thanks Teddy. It's just… umm, they, you know, they've asked us to turn our phones off of a night. So we don't get distracted. Or, you know, disturb others.'

'Oh, that's a bit harsh, isn't it, my love?'

'Thing is, Teddy, I kind of agree, you know? I really want to give this my best shot, so umm, yeah, I'm going to turn it off now. See you when I'm on the court. Bye.'

And she is gone. This can't be what she truly wants, but I must make the best of it. For her. For me. We barely exchange ten words the rest of the week. Every night, I continue to send her messages of support and encouragement. And tell her how much I miss her, that I cannot believe we are so close in distance, yet so far apart. I know she will be delighted when she turns her phone on each morning.

My beloved's team makes the finals. They only just lose.

At last, we can be together. Family and friends are part of a huge celebration dinner where they will announce the week's top players, along with those invited to try out for the national team.

Her name is not called out. Not for either. My beloved is devastated. I am devastated for her. I cannot bear to see her in such pain. But this is an opportunity! An end to all this distraction. I can take her away with me. This is truly for the best. For her. For me. I smile to myself at the thought.

Our eyes meet across that crowded room. She's being comforted by a teammate.

There's a strange look on her face. Oh, my poor love. She is so distressed. It's now that she truly needs the support only I can give her.

I have to hold her upright as we leave the function. I tell her how upset I am for her. 'Bullshit. You're a manipulative fucking creep, is what you are.' She must be very drunk. Why else would she say such a thing?

'But–'

'You know, your constant calls and messages and attention-seeking all this week didn't help at all. Or was that your aim all along?'

Oh my love, you don't mean this.

'No no no, of course not. You absolutely should have been picked. I never ever meant to distract you, my love. You know you mean the world to me. I love you so much. I would never do anything to hurt you. To harm you.'

'Whatever.' She shrugs off my arm, walks apart, arms crossed, a sulky child frown spoiling that beautiful face.

We will sort this out. She will see I only ever want the best for her. Thankfully we will be driving alone tonight. So we can put all this behind us. She calls goodbye to her teammates as they are getting on the bus, and we go to my car.

Before we leave, she turns to me. Tears are running down her cheeks. Oh my love, you do not have to apologise. Of course I forgive you.

'Teddy, it's over. I don't want to be with you anymore. I feel suffocated. You're always too close. You never give me any space. I'm flying to London next week. By myself. I don't want you to come.'

No. She doesn't mean this. She's not thinking straight. Or perhaps she is. She's met someone else. She's lying. She's my soulmate. How could she lie like this? How could she ever be with another? She's my soulmate. No one else can look after her like I can.

The way back to town is along a quiet country road, with many bends and sharp corners. But I know this car. I've driven this road many times this past week. I know it so well.

'Slow down, you're going way too fast. Teddy, what are you doing. Teddy, you're frightening me.'

Trees line the road, towering overhead. It will be quick, for both of us. For the best. Beyond the long straight ahead of us, the road curves into darkness. I press my foot down as hard as I can.

'Jo, I love you. I can't live without you. I can't bear to think of you with anyone else. They can never care for you like I can.'

Soulmates. Together. Forever.

Who You Callin' Old?

Denise Kramarczuk

There's a knock on the door of my room. It's Father Benedict, hell bent on saving my soul.

I've told him a thousand times it's a lost cause, but he keeps turning up. I sometimes feel it's his soul he's trying to save.

These priests, HA! What a joke! With all that talk of hellfire and damnation, they should be the one's worried. Perhaps they are and that's why he's always here. Come back another day I tell him... or not...I'm not bothered. Oh, that's in my mind I tell him, I've not spoken in weeks.

He leaves saying he'll not return. Hallelujah!!

I'm left in peace at last, but it's short lived.

The nursing staff now enter. Here they come, so cheerful all the time and such bloody gossips - it's quite sickening. Oh Lordy here we go, who's in for a roasting today? They're speaking in hushed tones so it must be juicy. Who's that? Gerald? Yes, yes, I know Gerald, gentle hands, unlike some of them. They think I can't hear them but they're wrong, I hear every word. It turns out Gerald is gay, left his wife, and moved in with his boyfriend… poor woman. They should be ashamed of themselves. The things they get up to are enough to make a sailor blush, and I've known many a sailor…honestly! I could tell them a thing or two believe you me! But I was never one for chit chat, they all knew that. I was always telling them to hurry up and get out, especially the cleaners who only ever did half a job!

Anyway, I'm now being tossed and turned, washed and basted. I feel like a Christmas turkey by the time they're finished and I smell like one too at times. One of the girls likes to put lavender in my room as she reckons it's relaxing and will aid in my passing. Well, it hasn't helped so far…I'm still here!

I've really no idea what time it is most days. I go by smells and sounds. Morning is the smell of burnt toast and bacon. Lunchtime? Well, anything from roast chicken to boiled beef and cabbage. The rattle of trays and trolleys is endless throughout the daylight hours. Evening is the smell of egg sandwiches and chicken with mayonnaise, the good old standbys. Midnight? Whisky and coffee!!

Visitors turn up to see the other "inmates" as I like to call them. I hear them walking past, so cheerful and bubbly. What have they got to be happy about? Once a young child popped their head into my room, but was quickly whisked away by an apologetic parent. I no longer have visitors. My fault. I've pushed them all away, so far away.

I was… well, still am, a grumpy old woman. Just ask any of the staff. Never satisfied with my lot in life. 'Grass was always greener on the other side' kind of person. I kept pushing and pushing until eventually the visiting stopped, the phone by my bedside never rang. Oh, they've visited since they've known I'm dying, to say their goodbyes. I know that much, and very sweet they were too. Sweet. Not a word I would usually use or care for, but yes they were. Sweet. I just wish I could have made myself tell them I knew they were here and how much I loved and appreciated them. But it's all too late now.

I made life difficult. For them, for everyone. Never liked their choice of spouse, career, lifestyle – I was always critical. I would justify it by thinking it was for their own good. And the poor grandchildren, God I must have been the grandmother from hell. Where did that come from? I had the most doting grandparents. I should have taken heed of the old saying 'be nice to your kids, they get to choose your nursing home'. That horse has well and truly bolted.

I still remember the day I turned up in this place after months in hospital. All I wanted was a smoke and a scotch! I tried bribing the paramedics to get me some on the way here but they wouldn't be in it. Spoilsports. The kids greeted me with smiling faces, thrilled they'd found somewhere for me that was close to them. They wanted me to be happy, but I couldn't have been more disappointed and I didn't hide it. Nice room, water views and all the mod cons, but it wasn't what I wanted. Where was my kitchen, my lounge…my things? Oh, a few were around; photos, my favourite chair, a TV. They explained I was no longer able to care for myself and required high care. Really? What rubbish! Where did they get that idea?

Looking back, I should have answered the assessment questions in hospital more honestly, instead of dismissing them with a wave of my hand and a disinterested sigh. These things can come back to bite you they said, and they were right. Apparently the retirement village I was in previously had a party when they heard I wasn't returning.

So, here I lie, alone and waiting. I've wasted a lot of time and energy being angry and resentful and yet I can't even remember why I was like that. Yeah, sure, my upbringing was strict and it was during the war. My grandparents raised me, as my parents were in London. I got sent away but my brothers and younger sister stayed. Mum said they couldn't afford to feed me, but surely it was the youngest that should be sent away? Perhaps that was where it all started, those feelings of rejection. My relationship with Mum was great. I don't want to talk about my father.

I'm the only one left now, but not for much longer. I'm so sleepy. The sort of the feeling you get after a few wines….light headed…almost peaceful.

Oh..I must have dozed off. Wait a minute, what's that noise? What the hell is going on? What are you talking about, you stupid girl? …Push? Push? I can't push; I've been comatose for weeks!

My God! What's that bright light?

Ooohhhh. This must be it, the finale. The bright light, it really does exist!. Well, just relax and head towards it, I don't think I have much choice in the matter anyway. At least it's not flames!. Arrgghh! It's a tight squeeze! HEY! Get those things off my head! HEEYYY! That hurts… get your cold mitts off me!

Whoa, I would have thought that the journey to the great beyond would have been more…whimsical?

Errr…who are these people looking at me? It's all a bit blurry at the moment. Who in blazes are they?

"Awww. Look, he's sooo handsome. Looks just like your dad. And look at his wrinkled face, such an old soul."

What's that? Old soul? Who you callin' old? Hang on… HE?!

Done Readin'

Terry Mulhern

The headmaster of the King's Orphan School in Hobart Town strode from one side of the schoolroom to the other, hands clasped behind his back. The silence was only broken by the swish of his long black frock coat and his deliberate slow footfalls.

'Repeat after me,' he said, '"f" is for father.'

'Eff-is-for-fah-tha,' we responded in a monotone chorus.

'Not that many of you would know your fathers,' he muttered under his breath.

I should have been more wary that day. Not staring out the window.

'Michael Mulligan!'

I was jolted from my daydream. 'Me, sir?'

'Yes, you. Stand up. How many Michael Mulligans do you think there are?'

'Umm, two?' The stinging whack to the side of my head set my ear ringing.

'Indeed. But only one bog-Irish whoreson with that name in this schoolroom.' The headmaster snatched my slate, 'Dear Lord, what's this? The scratchings of a blind monkey? Inattentive, insolent, illegitimate and illiterate!'

The other boys' laughter stung almost as much as the blow from the headmaster. I bit my lip and struggled to hold back my sobs. Burning with anger and shame, I decided on the spot, I was done with writin' – and done with readin'.

The very next day, me and another lad were assigned laundry duty. We lugged the big wicker basket filled with piss-soaked blankets down the stone steps to the basement. The new washerwoman turned to us and smiled, 'And who might you two little soldiers be?'

'Billy Williams, missus,' chirped my companion.

'Well, good day to you Billy.' She turned to me, 'And you?'

'Michael Mulligan.'

'Michael Mulligan… That's a good Irish name that one. Do they call you Mick or Micky at all?'

'No. Just Michael. The other one gets called Micky, so as not to get us confused.'

'Well Michael, I'm pleased to make your acquaintance.'

The washerwoman helped us lift the basket and dump the reeking bedding into the steaming copper. 'I've known a fair few Mulligans in my time,' she said, with a wink to her assistant. 'Would you be knowin' the names of any of your relatives, Michael?'

'Umm, I've got a ma. But I can't remember her name.'

'Well, no doubt she's a pretty lass. Do you remember anythin' about her?'

I frowned, unable to conjure anything but a hint of her comforting scent. The washerwoman broke the awkward silence, 'What about where you and your ma are from?'

I stared past the washerwoman, through the high stone wall and out of the school, groping at mist and vapour. 'I don't remember.'

'I'm supposin' you was only a wean when you come here?'

As I nodded, I saw a long thin shadow slipping down the stairs. I stood bolt upright and shut my mouth.

'That's enough chit-chat, Doherty,' said the matron. 'You've got too much work to do to waste time conversing with this little bastard.'

The next week, I was assigned to government farm. I walked the length of the rows of cabbages, whistling as I swung my hoe and chipped out weeds. The autumn sun warmed my back. As I worked, a melodic warbling rang out from the mountain's forested foothills. I leant on my hoe and listened. Two native magpies took turn-about to chase each other's carolling. Doodle-doodle-deedle-doodle-do.

Five of the black-and-white birds swooped down from the trees and strutted across the grass in front of me. The two largest birds had glossy black chests and crisp markings. The biggest one had a brilliant white cape, while the other's cape was grey. Grey cape stopped, turned its head to the side, then stabbed its sharp beak into the turf and pulled out a wriggling grub. The three smaller birds with fluffy mottled plumage crowded around it, bobbing and squawking. Grey cape fed the grub to one.

That night, I lay awake in the dormitory, ignoring the scurrying rodents. Where was my ma? Did she ever think of me? I took myself back to the nursery at the Female Factory and strained to remember more. Try as I might, no face came to me. Then, on the very edge of sleep, she whispered in my ear, soothing me with a promise that, 'at sunset in the summertime, after we are done readin', we'll have eggs.'

It was an odd thing to remember. Just those few words. Not the run of the story, nor the taste of the eggs.

*

We emerged from the schoolroom and lined up.

'...Jones, Abernathy, Stevenson, government farm. Smith and Blackthorn, laundry.'

'Beggin' your pardon ma'am,' I said, 'Jimmy Blackthorn's taken ill. The headmaster sent him to the infirmary. But I'll take his place, ma'am.'

'Why so eager for laundry, Mulligan?' said the matron, 'Are you preparing for a career on the tubs? You'd look pretty in a bonnet and apron.'

The other boys laughed. I felt my face flush. 'No ma'am,' I said, 'I just thought Charlie could do with help.'

'How very charitable. Go on then. But I've got my eye on you.'

We collected the soiled bedding from the dormitory and headed for the basement.

'Slow down,' whined Charlie, 'if we finish too quick, we'll just get somethin' else to do.'

'Hurry up,' I said, 'I've got my reasons.'

Clouds of steam and laughter floated up from the laundry as we brought the basket thudding down the steps. 'Hello lads,' said the washerwoman.

As we tipped the blankets into the copper, I whispered to her, 'You know my ma, don't you?'

'Maybe.'

'I've remembered somethin' she told me. From when I was a littlun.'

'Good lad. Hang back when we're done.'

We hauled the last load of wet washing out to the lines. I looked down each of the long grey flapping rows for the washerwoman. She was at the end of the last one, adjusting a wooden prop to make sure nothing dragged in the dirt. She looked up and beckoned to me. I glanced around and scurried towards her, meeting her broad smile with my own.

'Why so joyful, Mulligan?' said the matron, appearing like a spectre from among the washing. 'The Lord may love a boy who's happy in his work, but I smell a rat.' She turned to the washerwoman, 'What're you up to Doherty? If you're using him to thieve, I'll have you up before the magistrate.'

'No, ma'am. Nothin' like that. I promise. I just took a fancy to this one. He reminds me of my own lad – who died a terrible death at his age. Oh, it was awful. He was gripped by a tremendous fever and great boils burst all over him...'

'Enough! I've no interest in the death throes of your purulent offspring. Empty your pockets, the pair of you.'

I silently thanked my guardian angel all I had on me were two coloured pebbles and the long front tooth of a kangaroo. The washerwoman had only her rosary beads.

The matron huffed in disappointment. 'If I detect the least sniff of malfeasance from you Doherty, you'll be back at the Factory so quick it'll make your head spin. And you, Master Mulligan, I'll be discussing you with the headmaster. I think other duties can be found for an eager worker like yourself.'

*

Snow lay heavy on the mountain top. Frost crackled under my feet. My arms ached. I lifted one bucket and then the other, tipping the stinking excrement into the cesspit. I tried not to gag. I picked up the other empty bucket and trudged back towards the privies. My mood was as low as the temperature. How could I let the washerwoman know what I'd remembered? God knows, I'd never get laundry duty ever again.

As I walked under the windows of the schoolroom, I heard one of the older boys reading aloud, 'Thus speaketh the Lord God of Israel, saying, write thee all the words that I have spoken unto thee in a book…'

I stopped and stared up, open mouthed.

*

Hot sun poured in on the rows of desks. We sweated like horses under the whip. The headmaster's chalk clacked and squeaked.

'Now, what are these letters I've written here?'

I thrusted my hand up. The headmaster ignored me.

'Yes, Walker.'

'They're the vowels, sir.'

'Good boy. Now, all of you, write a list of five words, one for each vowel "a-e-i-o" and "u". Every word must start with the letter "t" and have the vowel as the second letter.'

I thought for a moment then wrote "talk, tent, tilt, told, turn".

The headmaster walked behind me, leant over and with a shake of his head, muttered, 'The Lord moves in mysterious ways.'

Later, in the semi-darkness of the late summer twilight, I pulled my blanket up over my head. I squeezed the stub of a pencil out of the seam of my thin straw-filled mattress and unfolded the blank half-page I'd torn from a prayer book. I crossed myself – just in case it was a sin –

and wrote Ma's promise in careful large letters.

*

I rinsed the last plate and placed it on the rack to dry. When I pulled out the wooden plug, the greyish water gurgled as it ran from the washtub into a large pail.

'Excuse me, missus,' I said to the cook, 'shall I go and put this water on the garden?'

'Aye,' she said, 'but be quick about it. Then you can take these peelin's to the pigs.'

I hefted up the heavy bucket, staggered along the hall and out into the sunshine. I moved quickly along the beds, pouring water on the plants as I went. I stopped near the small open window that looked down into the basement. I could hear the washerwoman's cheerful chatter echoing up. I look left and right, then peered in.

She had her back to me. In her hands was the enormous wooden paddle she used to stir the garments in the copper. I took from my pocket a rock, around which I'd tied my note. I tapped it on the window frame. She looked up. I was about to drop the rock through the window when she held up her hand and shook her head at me.

'Beth,' she called to her unseen assistant, 'would you be a darlin' and go and get some more soap from the storeroom? We'll be needin' it soon enough.'

The washerwoman waited a few moments, then looked up at me and nodded. I tossed the rock. It clattered onto the floor and skidded under a trestle table against the wall. She hustled over, bent down, looked under the table and reached out her arm.

'What are you looking for, Doherty?' said the matron. My heart sank and I dropped flat on the ground below the window.

'Oh ma'am,' said the washerwoman, 'there was a rat. It scurried under this table. It was ever so big. I'll crawl under here and see if there's a hole.'

'Good Lord! Get up, you stupid woman.'

'I won't be a moment, ma'am. It's just that I'm a touch stuck. It's the rheumatism in me back. If I stretch my arms out, it usually goes away...'

The seconds that ticked by felt like hours.

'That's got it ma'am,' called the washerwoman loudly, 'right as rain.'

*

Kathleen Doherty spied Mary Mulligan across the dusty catholic churchyard. Mary was just visible through the throng of red-coated Irish soldiers competing for conversation with the prettiest convict girls. Kathleen muscled her way through, took Mary by the arm and led her aside. Kathleen slipped my crumpled scrap of paper into Mary's hand.

'This is for you. It's from him.'

Mary nodded as she unfolded the page. 'Do you know what it says?'

'No more than you.'

'Old Brigid O'Shea, then?'

'Aye, she may charge like a wounded bull, but she knows how to keep her trap shut.'

The old woman was sheltering in the narrow strip of shade, on the southern side of the rude barn-like wooden chapel.

'Brigid, would you be able to help me?' said Mary.

'You know the score Mulligan, tuppence to read, sixpence to write.' Mary passed her the slip of paper and the coins.

'Whose writin' is this?'

'It's a message from my boy,' said Mary. 'Well, I think he's my boy.'

'How old is he?'

'If it's him, he'd be nine, last September.'

'Hmm, not too bad, then. You know he says you used to read to him.'

'Me? No, that can't be right. I can't read!' Mary turned to Kathleen, her face aghast. 'Why would he say that? When I cared for him in the nursery, I told him about where he comes from. But I never read to him. How could I? Oh Kathleen, do you think he's the wrong one? You said there was two Michael Mulligans.'

Kathleen put her arm around Mary. 'Brigid, what's he written? Read it to us. Every word.'

The old woman took a deep breath, 'When-we-are-done-readin'-at-sun-set-in-the summer-time-we-will-have-eggs.'

'Oh dear,' said Kathleen, shaking her head.

Mary burst out laughing. Brigid and Kathleen looked at her like she'd gone mad. Mary laughed and jumped and clapped.

'He's my boy and he remembers me!' Mary hugged Brigid and kissed her on both her wrinkled cheeks, turned and grabbed Kathleen's hands and swung her around.

'What, how?'

'Done readin', Kathleen. Don't you see? I'm from Doonreaghan. The poor lamb has just remembered it a touch wrong.'

'And eggs in the summertime?'

Mary laughed, 'I used to tell him how in the summer, from up on the cliffs, I'd watch the sun set over the Skelligs.'

Now Kathleen laughed too.

Kathleen held Mary – my Ma – in a long embrace. 'Keep out of trouble, Pet,' said Kathleen, 'and soon you'll get your ticket of leave. Then you'll be able to see him. After that, all you need do is marry a freeman, and they'll let you have him back.'

I know all this because Ma told me about that day over and over. She said my words carried her on angel's wings, back to a Kerry clifftop, high above the sea. Gulls lifted by the updraft swirled around her. She watched the sun slip behind the silhouette of two distant, pyramid-shaped islands. Tears rolled down her cheeks as she described to me a different pair of strong encircling arms.

'Will you come again tomorrow, Mary Mulligan?' he asked her.

Ma drew his face to hers and kissed him. 'Michael Fitzgerald, there's nothin' in this world that could stop me.'

But Ma was wrong. The constables came for her that night. In court, Lady Fitzgerald's footman swore Ma stole a pair of silver candlesticks worth £10. The filthy liar. Ma said they were pewter and never worth more than six shillings. She was transported before she even showed.

If I ever get to Ireland, I know I won't be welcome in my father's house. But Ma and I are together now and that's family enough for me.

About the cover of Soul

The artwork used on the cover of *Soul* was created by writer and artist Denise Kramarczuk who lives in Tolmie, just up the hill from Mansfield.

Denise also has a story published in the *Soul* anthology 'Who you Callin' Old' so it's doubly exciting to have her artwork adorning the cover.

Artist statement

Scientists believe we are made of atoms and stardust, evolved over millions of years. But what of our soul? To many, the soul provides us our identity, personality and memories – it is our authentic self, our essence. Forever immortal, it continues on after our physical death. Beliefs as to its journey after our passing are as numerous as the stars. Perhaps there is where we should look for an answer.

Ancient Mayans and Indigenous American tribes believe the soul travels on, long after it leaves our body. The soul travels along a mystic highway, a spirit trail if you wish. It traverses the Milky Way, past and through black holes before arriving at a place of perpetual peace and happiness. It would seem that the ancient civilizations may have been aware of a pathway leading from our galaxy to an alternate realm of existence.

It's a lovely thought, isn't it? My painting, 'A soul's pilgrimage', seeks to capture this journey through the stars.

Denise Kramarczuk
Tolmie, 2023

Thank you to the Friends of Mansfield Library

The Friends of Mansfield Library Inc (FOML) have generously provided Mansfield Readers and Writers with funds to support the publication of this anthology.

Since 1991, the FOMLs have promoted, supported and advocated for the Mansfield Library. They believe in the importance of libraries as community hubs and places of ideas.

How the FOMLs raise funds for Mansfield Library

The FOML fund-raising efforts include running a preloved book shop (the Little Shop of Good Reads) and regular book sales aligned with the Mansfield Bush Markets.

In 2022 and 2023 they applied successfully for a community grant with Community Bank Mansfield & District.

How the FOMLs use the funds they raise

Thanks to the support of Community Bank Mansfield & District, the

FOMLs have provided a self-serve book check out kiosk at Mansfield Library.

Funds raised by the FOMLs are used for resources and activities that contribute to or align with the Library's programs.

For example, the FOMLs have hosted authors visits, run a Mad Hatters' Tea party during Seniors Festival, and held a Harry Potter themed children's activity. They contribute to Library activities such as the children's Christmas Party, and other holiday programs and Armchair Travel presentations. In conjunction with the CWA, the FOML's have funded the purchase of items to be included in Maternal and Child Health Baby Book Bags. The FOMLs also advocate on issues related to our Library.

How to get involved

The FOMLS always welcome new members to help fund raise and organise events in support of the Library's programs. You can reach them by visiting the Little Shop of Good Reads on Curia Street across from the Mansfield Shire offices, or connect on Facebook.

www.ingramcontent.com/pod-product-compliance
Lightning Source LLC
Chambersburg PA
CBHW030635120726
47904CB00006B/2160